Miss Parker's Ponies

Miss Parker's Ponies

Victoria Hinshaw

THORNDIKE
CHIVERS

This Large Print edition is published by Thorndike Press®, Waterville, Maine USA and by BBC Audiobooks, Ltd, Bath, England.

Published in 2004 in the U.S. by arrangement with Zebra Books, an imprint of Kensington Publishing Corp.

Published in 2004 in the U.K. by arrangement with the author.

U.S. Hardcover 0-7862-6534-5 (Romance)
U.K. Hardcover 0-7540-9646-7 (Chivers Large Print)

The text of this Large Print edition is unabridged.
Other aspects of the book may vary from the original edition.

Set in 16 pt. Plantin by Minnie B. Raven.

Printed in the United States on permanent paper.

British Library Cataloguing-in-Publication Data available

Library of Congress Cataloging-in-Publication Data

Hinshaw, Victoria.
    Miss Parker's ponies / Victoria Hinshaw.
      p. cm.
    ISBN 0-7862-6534-5 (lg. print : hc : alk. paper)
    1. Napoleonic Wars, 1800–1815 — Veterans — Fiction.
  2. Women horse owners — Fiction. 3. London (England)
— Fiction. 4. Large type books. I. Title.
PS3608.I578M57 2004
  813'.6—dc22   2004045952

Miss Parker's Ponies

One

"Oh, come look! I think they are here."

Her cheeks rosy with excitement, her blue eyes shining, Miss Caroline Parker rushed into the spacious drawing room of Sunnyslope's grand mansion. As usual, Caro was completely unmindful of her golden hair tumbling free of her half-tied ribbons. Nor did a sense of proper deportment curb her rush to reach the tall Palladian window overlooking the pebbled drive.

"Hurry, Isabel," Caroline called to her cousin. "They have finally arrived."

"At last. It is too exciting!"

"Later than I expected." Caroline peered intently at the three men bringing their horses to a stop outside the pillared portico. The riders wore heavy coats against the chill of the February day. One was her cousin Lord Edward Mortimer, at twenty considered by both Caroline and his sister Isabel to be an utter scapegrace, albeit dearly loved. The other two were strangers, though clearly clad in the fashion of gentlemen of substance.

Her brown eyes gleaming, Isabel pressed Caroline's hand. "Is everything ready?"

Caroline accorded her a conspiratorial grin. "Yes. Ned and his friends will have quite a surprise." Her laughter bubbled up as lightly as tinkling bells when she visualized the approaching scene.

"You have to change. Should you not hurry?" Isabel asked.

Caroline's eyes were fastened on the wide shoulders and lean build of one stranger as he swung down from his saddle. He stroked the neck of his mount, a tall and rangy bay, before he handed the reins to a groom. Doffing his hat, the young man ran his fingers through his russet brown hair, leaving it tousled and wavy, then turned his attention to brushing the road dust from his shoulders. When he moved to speak to the others, Caroline noticed a slight limp to his gait. He definitely favored his right leg.

Caroline immediately guessed his identity. "Ned got the Ogden brothers to come! The taller one has a limp."

Isabel concurred. "Then he must be Thomas Ogden. He is wickedly handsome, just as Ned promised. Now I believe those stories Ned told about Captain Ogden's escapades."

"Do not be wig-witted. He looks quite ordinary to me." Caroline dared not admit Captain Ogden was disturbingly like the debonair heroes of several recent novels, his forehead noble, his features perfectly chiseled, his bearing fittingly patrician. Even his expression carried the hint of a darkly sardonic temperament. Or was this just her imagination?

"I find him excessively good-looking," Isabel declared.

"I suppose some might find him attractive. And he no doubt knows it." Caroline recalled Ned's boasts of his friendship with the elder Ogden brother. Sadly, she thought, those tales had more to do with the captain's exploits at London gaming tables than with his service to the crown.

Isabel could not contain her enthusiasm. "This is perfect! Ned says Captain Ogden is quite the rakehell, the ideal buyer for his team of blacks."

Mention of the horses brought Caroline's attention back to their plans. "Ned will be beside himself when we're finished with him, absolutely mad with rage."

Something he heard outside brought Thomas Ogden a smile, a rather raffish smile, Caroline noted. That one would have few lonesome moments, with that crooked grin at the ready. She was not so green that she lacked an understanding of how the ladies of London might comfort a hero home from the Peninsular Wars.

Instead of running to greet the party, Caro and Isabel stayed out of sight as the men entered the foyer, met by Plummer, Sunnyslope's capable, if long-suffering, butler.

"Your father is not at home this morning, milord. But perhaps you and your guests would have coffee in the breakfast room . . ."

Ned interrupted the butler, his voice quivering in his anticipation of exhibiting the team. "Yes, Plummer. Coffee for Captain Thomas Ogden and Mr. Simon Ogden. And don't disturb Mother yet. Tell the stables we will see the pair at eleven."

The clock had just chimed ten. Caroline had plenty of time to prepare for the delicious caper she and Isabel planned.

"Is everything ready?" Isabel whispered for the second time.

"Yes. Everything. We are sure to have great success."

"Ned will never be able to top this!" Isabel wore a mischievous smile.

Another thrill of excitement tickled Caroline's spine, and she suppressed a giggle as she imagined dear old Ned's reaction. She rubbed her hands together, trying to picture the look of astonishment on his face when their prank began.

Leaving Isabel to collect her little brother Henry and sister Becky, fellow conspirators in harassing their elder brother, Caroline skipped up the stairway, hurrying toward her room.

"Miss Caroline," the housekeeper called, "Lady Barstow asks you to attend her in the sitting room."

"Now? I was about to . . ."

"There has been a letter from your mother, I believe," Mrs. Wood interrupted.

At once, Caroline dashed to Aunt Letitia. How she missed her dear mother so far away in Sweden. She prayed the letter forecast a visit from Lady Clarissa Parker very soon. But when she entered the sitting room, she was thoroughly puzzled by Aunt Letitia's look of acute distress.

Fanning herself with a rumpled lace hankie, the plump and lovable Countess of Barstow reclined on a velvet couch, biting her lip and frowning. She waved Caroline to a seat, held up the letter, and said in a trembling voice, "Your mama will arrive any day now."

11

"Wonderful! I have not seen her in almost a year." Caroline found no one more beautifully petite, accomplished, and adorable than her darling mama. Caroline had pleaded to accompany her back to the Swedish royal capital when their mourning period ended for Sir Quentin, but Lady Clarissa would not hear of it. She had promised the British ambassador she would continue her duties as hostess for the embassy just as she had when her husband was alive. Caroline had remained with her cousins here at Sunnyslope, the family home of Clarissa's own youth.

"So very disappointing," Lady Barstow said, sniffing. "I fear I have sadly let her down."

"I do not understand."

"She is coming to prepare you to go to London in April, for the Season, and I know she will expect . . ."

"The Season!" Caroline exclaimed. "I thought we all agreed that Isabel and I would have our come outs together some day." Caroline's eagerness to see her mother was suddenly a bit clouded.

"Your mama is quite insistent. She wants you to make your curtsy this year. Your Aunt Augusta has agreed to assist."

"Oh no." Caroline dreaded any contact

with Lady Augusta Stolper, her mother's elder sister. Despite the fact Aunt Letitia's husband, Jeremy Mortimer, Earl of Barstow, was the formal head of the family, Aunt Augusta had long ruled with her haughty and overbearing ways. "Why would Mama do this to us?"

"I declare I cannot comprehend. And you are distressingly ill prepared, my dear. Your mama will think me a complete cabbage head for the way I have neglected your instruction. Your music, your French, your needlework. I have let you set them all aside."

"Let me ring for some tea, Aunt Letitia. You look thoroughly overset." As she carried out her task, Caroline considered her lack of preparation and knew the fault was hers alone. Aunt Letitia was correct. Caroline was certainly not prepared to enter Society on any level at all, much less be presented at Court.

Aunt Letitia continued to dither. "Augusta will say I have woefully botched my responsibilities. She will complain to Jeremy, poor man. I have heard her accusations before, letting the family down and all that. And she calls me 'that goose you married.'" Letitia's tears flowed freely. "Where has the time gone, with no

13

dancing instructor or piano master? You will make a cake of yourself, and Augusta will blame everything on me."

"We have to change Mama's mind. There is no need for me to have a Season this year."

"Oh, dear," Letitia wailed. "I fear she is quite determined." She held the letter out to Caroline, who took it and sank onto the window seat to read.

When she finished, Caroline gazed out of the window sadly. Was she ready to give up her youth, to lose the independence of life here at Sunnyslope? Her easygoing years with the Earl and Countess of Barstow were the opposite of her life as a young child. Almost from birth Caroline had traveled to the diplomatic capitals of Europe with her parents. At age ten, she came to Sunnyslope to benefit from the wholesome Berkshire countryside, just as her mother had as a child. As strange as the ways of the Mortimer family seemed at first, soon she loved Sunnyslope. Now this new plan meant the end of her freedom to train her ponies, to drive over the estate without a groom, to picnic with her cousins beside the river after escaping their feckless governess.

Aunt Letitia sighed mournfully. "Come

and pour the tea, dear. I declare I am too trembly to do a thing."

Caroline acted automatically, her mind far away as she handed a brimming cup to her aunt.

"Caroline, look at your hands. Your nails are all torn and ragged."

Caroline nodded, her dismal thoughts transcending mere fingernails. Having a Season was just the beginning. Mama not only intended to bring her out; Lady Clarissa fully expected to see her daughter wed this very year. *It is time for Caroline to be settled,* Mama had written.

The thought was enough to make Caroline run off to America. Who cared about chapped hands with a whole lifetime at stake? A husband, indeed! She had no experience of men other than family. Marriage was something to think of in the future, not now while she so treasured her independence.

"I think you have done no more than a tiny corner of your sampler," Aunt Letitia moaned.

If she was not facing the prospect of utter doom, Caroline might be sympathetic to her aunt's complaints. Lady Barstow had never wielded much control of her household, especially where her high-spirited offspring were concerned, and Caroline had learned to fit into the family pattern in the eight years she had lived with her cousins.

"We have to change her mind, that is all. I simply refuse to go to London for the Season, and I certainly do not plan to marry anybody. At least not in the near future."

Caroline's expression of defiance brought new moans from her aunt. "What have I done to deserve this? None of my children are obedient and respectful, not even you, Caroline, who should have learned better from your mother."

"Please do not cry, Aunt Letitia. We must concentrate on changing Mama's mind." But even as she spoke, Caroline felt the hopelessness of the task. In her much more graceful way, Clarissa showed every bit as much determination and strength of backbone as the imperious Augusta. Together, they would be invincible. Aunt Letitia would be of no help whatsoever.

Caroline's mood of merry anticipation disappeared, but for the sake of Isabel, Henry, and Becky, she had better go change. Later she would figure a way out, or she would end up wed to some pompous sapskull chosen by her Aunt Augusta.

★ ★ ★

"Do hope these nags are worth the time," Thomas Ogden drawled, a teasing undertone in his voice. He leaned back in his chair and flicked an imaginary speck of dust from the sleeve of his perfectly tailored coat of dark blue superfine. The two younger men across the table from him were too excited to present the cool and polished façade of London gentlemen, and Thomas was rather amused.

"Think of what you could wager on them." Simon wavered between the eagerness of his friend Ned and the detachment of his brother, Thomas.

Ned nearly burst to show off his blacks. "Worth plenty of guineas to a fellow challengin' every comer on the Brighton road. You could match your income at cards, Tom."

Thomas shrugged and sipped his coffee. He really was not interested in the horses. This brief visit to Sunnyslope was merely a convenient stop on his journey to accommodate an urgent summons from his mother. But he wanted to indulge Ned and Simon. After all, they held him in some degree of awe, due primarily to Thomas's many successes at London gaming tables, not to mention his record in the war. The debilities left from his wounds gave a slight weakness to his leg, which, with his dark good looks, caused him to receive fawning attention from the muslin set. In the eyes of Ned and Simon, such regard was particularly enviable. They would learn differently someday, Thomas supposed, once the two young sprigs had another year or two of polish.

"Difficult, don't you know, to find a truly black pair." Ned nervously smoothed his saffron-striped waistcoat. "Their color is splendid, quite exceptional."

Thomas nodded, his mind far away. Strange that his mother should send for him so soon after Christmas and with the February roads so chancy. Anger at some stray gossip about him must be Lady Elizabeth's reason for requiring his presence. But no sense in worrying. He had a full day's ride before he had to face her and attend to her wrath.

"Speedy and flashy goers, too, spanking fine!" Ned rubbed his hands together in his impatience. "They'll be 'round in front at eleven sharp, the finest cattle in five counties!"

Ned's father, the Earl of Barstow, bred fine horses of matchless quality. Thomas knew Ned was anxious to carry on the family tradition, to show off his pair as the pride of his father's stud. Several fellows of his acquaintance in town were likely buyers, Thomas mused. He'd see that Ned's treasures found an appropriate home.

By eleven, Ned had nearly jumped out of his skin in anticipation of the impending exhibition. The instant the clock finally chimed, he immediately pushed back his chair and started down the hall. Thomas could not help chuckling. Ned's stiff collar points stabbed his cheeks as he tried to turn and talk to them. But apparently no discomfort so minor could stop his constant flow of words.

"Both sire and dam are descended from the Darley Arabian . . ." How many times had Ned reiterated the bloodlines, Thomas wondered.

". . . the sire was a winner at Newmarket three years in a row, and both dams were daughters of highly regarded studs . . ."

When they reached the broad portico overlooking the spacious park and circular gravel drive, Thomas shielded his eyes from the bright sky of the crisp and windy afternoon. From the rear of the house, he heard hooves crunching on the gravel. Ned clasped his hands together fervently and poked Thomas with his elbow, unable to resist one more boast. "Just you see now, they're simply top o' the trees."

Thomas watched as the pair raced around the corner at a full gallop. Sunlight glinted on ebony coats and shining black harness. Bits of gravel flying beneath their feet, they circled the drive at breakneck speed, driven by a young groom in maroon livery.

But instead of invoking a properly admiring phrase, Thomas found himself smothering a howl of laughter. He blinked twice and looked again. What he saw was a team of ponies! The fleet-footed pair skimming the gravel could not have been more than half size, however perfect in every other way. The curricle was a miniature, and even the top-hatted driver seemed diminutive as the handsome equipage flew around the grassy verge and fountain.

At first Thomas thought the joke was on him, but a quick glance at Ned revealed the total astonishment on his face. This tiny team's arrival must be a complete surprise.

"Those damnable little nags," Ned sputtered.

Simon was openmouthed in surprise and amazement. "By Jupiter! What kind of caper-wits do you take us for?"

"I say, Ned. Your wretched cattle seem to have shrunk!" Thomas strove to maintain a semblance of composure.

Ned's face burned crimson with fury, and he shook his fist as he watched the ponies sprint past on yet another circuit of the drive. No longer able to preserve their aplomb, Thomas and Simon broke out in great whoops of laughter at the bizarre scene.

The tiny team was as fine as any Thomas had ever seen, simply half as large. They certainly had fire and spirit, and the entire rig looked perfect in every regard except stature.

Abruptly Ned leaped down the steps and recklessly jumped into the path of the onrushing team, howling his rage and humiliation. Startled, Thomas lunged after him, sure the galloping pair would crush Ned. But, with great skill, the driver swerved the team and avoided both the fist-shaking young man and his would-be savior. In a spray of pebbles, the team of ponies swooped away and disappeared again behind the house.

Thomas laughed, at first in relief, then at the face before him. Purple with rage, Ned seemed oblivious to his close brush with disaster. His angry muttering was drowned out by Simon's cries of merriment, and Thomas doubled over in roars of elation. Ned mumbled something about his cousin, but both Ogdens were too weak with laughter to listen.

"Handsome cattle indeed," Simon said, giving Ned a cuff on the shoulder.

"Just the thing for racing in Hampstead," Thomas agreed.

"We'll challenge every nob in London," Simon went on.

Ned looked mortified, hardly appreciative of the Ogden brothers' amusement.

Thomas struggled to find his voice. "Highly divertin' exhibition, Ned."

Before Ned could speak, another team came into view, this time a splendid pair of tall and fiery blacks, as so long promised. Ned's expression changed instantly from a mixture of anger and humiliation to good cheer. "Here they are! I told you they were prime."

Thomas, his stomach aching from laughter, could only agree. "Prime as they are, the first pair would make the bigger splash in the park."

But Ned was too busy pointing out the finer points of his blacks' conformation and bragging about their action to discuss the pony team. His consequence some-what restored, Ned motioned the driver to stop the team. "Here, have a turn," he said, offering the reins to Thomas.

Carefully Thomas pulled himself up to replace the lanky tiger on the curricle seat and set the blacks at a trot down the driveway, leaving Simon to join Ned in rhapsodizing over the horses. Thomas laughed again to himself. Someone had pulled a fine and proper joke on Ned. Halfway to the estate's gate, he turned the team and returned up the drive to the house.

"Your turn," he said to Simon as he alit from the curricle. Ned's steady stream of chatter continued as the two younger men climbed aboard and set off down the drive.

Thomas was more curious about the po-nies than he was interested in the horses. It was not often one saw such finely turned out ponies, with all the action and dash of full-size teams. Other than his childhood pet at Pemstead, a gentle roan too fat for more than ambling, Thomas had little con-tact with the miniature equines. Leaning only a bit on his walking stick, he headed to the stables for a closer look.

As he skirted the kitchen garden, he heard laughter from the direction of the stables. So the servants found Ned's embarrassment a point of merriment. Apparently a cheeky crew! From the sound of girlish giggles, even the kitchen maids enjoyed the joke.

Perched on the miniature curricle, Caroline untangled the reins again for her young cousin Henry.

"We are almost finished cooling the ponies," she said. "So turn them around and head back to the stable. Gently, now." She reached up to tuck a few stray ringlets back under her hat. You could never tell who might be looking out of the upstairs windows of the big house, and she certainly did not want to cause inquiries. Better to appear some anonymous groom in the estate livery.

"When you have built your confidence, you will be a top whip. Just pay attention to the ponies."

"I did not expect driving to be so difficult."

Caroline grinned. "You have to be patient and practice. You can drive the cool-off again tomorrow if you wish."

For over a year, Caroline's training sessions with two teams of ponies had been her first priority. She took pride in her accomplishments, even if the first real showing took place before strangers as part of a practical joke. Now she needed to get this particular team unhitched and her clothes changed before Uncle Jeremy saw her. He understood, even encouraged her pony training, but if he saw her dressed in estate livery . . .

Caroline looked toward the stable yard. "The girls are waiting for us. I hope they found a place to see everything."

Henry sat up a mite straighter. "Isabel would not have missed old Ned's fits for anything."

Isabel and Becky waved to them from the end of the long lane between the stables and sheds. Isabel was already a willowy young woman, taller than Caroline, though two years younger. Rebecca, at eight, was the baby of the family, chubby and adorable, with a sweet disposition to match. Now their faces showed triumph and eagerness to relive the moment of victory.

"You are doing fine," Caroline said to Henry. "Keep them at a steady pace."

This particular pair of ponies, Oberon and Titania, was born of the two mares she so carefully chose when she first decided to spend her annual allowance on horses. Or rather, on ponies, for Uncle Jeremy found her original idea of owning and breeding horses much too unladylike. Ponies somehow met with his approval, and now she had six in all.

When they reached his sisters, Henry stopped the ponies with an exaggerated, "Whoa."

"We were peeking out the window," Isabel said, "and Ned's face got so red, I thought he was choking."

Becky's big grin confirmed her glee. "He must be angry with us."

Henry carefully climbed down from the curricle, then held the ponies' heads.

Isabel continued. "Captain Ogden and his brother were laughing excessively."

"Both of them are very handsome," Becky said.

"I am afraid I did not notice." Caroline did not tell the whole truth. She had heard Captain Ogden laughing in a deep baritone voice that made her toes wiggle.

Caroline went to Oberon's head and scratched his ears as the groom Will unhitched the rig. "Good fella'," she murmured as the pony leaned into her touch.

Isabel followed, her voice a whisper to avoid the ears of Henry and Becky. "Of course, Simon Ogden is terribly immature,

26

just like Ned. But the captain is ever so experienced, quite the dashing rakehell, Ned says. I wonder if he has a mistress."

Caroline feigned disinterest. "What do you know about such things? Nonsense, Isabel. I never heard anything so silly."

"Who is silly?" Henry asked.

"Why are you whispering?" Becky was indignant at being left out of the conversation.

"We were laughing about how furious Ned was," Isabel said.

They all four joined hands and laughed together.

Thomas followed the sounds of laughter to the rear of the house. As he rounded the corner to the stable yard, his mouth dropped open in surprise.

An unlikely assortment of personages clustered around the ponies and miniature curricle. The liveried driver embraced a young lady of about sixteen years, her dress clearly signaling that she was a Mortimer daughter, not a servant. Beside them was an appealing little girl with a rabbit fur muff. A young man, little more than a child really, frolicked about them singing, "Old Ned, lead head."

What kind of a bumblebroth was this?

Poor Ned, if he had to live in the middle of such mismanaged chaos.

The burly groom unhitching the curricle shook his head and spoke without listeners. "Don' know what the master will say. Such nonsense'll be trouble, 'tis for certain sure."

The driver detached himself from the taller girl. "Do not trouble yourself, Will. I shall take care no repercussions fall upon you or the other hands."

Then, to Thomas's utter amazement, the driver doffed the hat to reveal a knot of honey blond curls. Despite the snug breeches and brass-buttoned livery jacket, he saw the driver was a female, a quite lovely young woman with a wide smile and pink cheeks. As she shook her head, her golden curls cascaded down and loose.

Thomas grinned to himself. The caper was a family escapade, not a case of misbehaving help. Quite an amusing little incident to tease a brother with, he thought. Perhaps even good for some familial extortion at the right moments. Years ago, he and his own brothers had searched their youthful brains for methods of ridiculing one another, but never had they come up with anything quite this elaborate. He took a few steps nearer their circle.

"Your skill with the ribbons is most impressive," Thomas said to the driver. His smile widened at the amazement on all their faces when they noticed his presence. "I am Thomas Ogden, brother of Ned's classmate Simon." He thought a slight blush deepened on the young lady's rosy cheeks as she lifted her sky blue eyes to his. Astonishingly pretty, he thought, though quite obviously chagrined at his presence. As a few more curls trailed down from her topknot to fan across her face, a slight frown creased her forehead.

The smallest girl bounced up to perform the introductions. "I am Becky Mortimer, Captain Ogden. Pleased to make your acquaintance. This is my brother Henry, my sister Isabel, and my cousin Caroline Parker." Her words accompanied a wave at the young lady driver.

"Nicely said," Thomas observed. "Those are very fine ponies, if not quite what your brother was expecting to show off."

"Old Ned is much too high in the instep now that he is supposed to be at Oxford," Henry said. "Caroline thought we could give him a proper set down."

"I would say Miss Parker was successful in her efforts," Thomas replied, turning to look at the erstwhile driver. She met his gaze with a barely suppressed grin, her enormous blue eyes bright with mischief.

"Caroline is a dab hand with ponies," Henry went on.

"And so fetchingly costumed." Thomas looked directly at her breeches, smoothly molded to her legs and slender hips, which made an eye-filling display. "I am gratified to find all the scenery here at Sunnyslope presents a most pleasing vista."

Caroline sniffed at his remark and turned abruptly to help the groom unharness the ponies. She knew her cheeks were burning in humiliation. Whatever she wore, he had colossal nerve making such a tasteless remark. Pointedly ignoring Thomas, she softly crooned her praise to the handsome creatures as she worked.

"Caroline trained the ponies herself," Becky chirped.

"A most excellent avocation," the captain said. "Though unique, even for a country miss. Quite as unusual as your ensemble." He finished with a bow to Caroline.

With an attempt at perfect dignity, Caroline walked into the tack room and closed the door. She felt thoroughly humiliated. Ned had bragged for months about his friendship with London's most accomplished rakes. How could she find this one so very handsome at the very same time he scrutinized her legs? Why, his eyes had unmistakably been fixed upon her bottom. No indeed, she had not missed that look, not quite a leer, but certainly not the way a gentleman should admire a lady. Her fingers shook as she unfastened the livery coat and vest, turning to contemplate herself in the looking glass placed for her use after sessions with the ponies.

Her face flamed in embarrassment at her reflection. The breeches and knee stockings hugged her like a second skin.

Good Lord, no wonder he had stared!

Quickly she changed into her morning gown of pale lavender muslin and hung away the livery. She refused to be intimidated by the way he had ogled her. A true gentleman would not have noticed her legs at all.

When she heard the voices of Ned and Simon returning, Caroline swiftly left the stable and hurried to the house the roundabout way through the orchard. One thing for sure, she would keep well out of the way for the remainder of Captain Thomas Ogden's visit. He would leave tomorrow morning, thank heavens.

Two

"I knew it. Thomas Ogden gambles, and he wins piles of money." Isabel closed the door of Caroline's room behind her.

"How do you know?" Caroline stood before the cheval glass trying to arrange her hair. For some reason, its usual slapdash style did not satisfy her this afternoon.

Isabel's tone was both admiring and conspiratorial. "Ned and Simon told me. He even won the horse he is riding. At a place called Watier's in London. And he was wounded in the war. He is seven and twenty, the perfect age for you, Caroline. Or even for me."

"You are being a ninnyhammer, Isabel. We should be preparing for dinner, not gossiping like a pair of village milkmaids."

Dressed in her very best muslin, Caroline led the way downstairs. How could she refine on their rude fribble of a guest when she faced the total disruption of her life? What she needed was time; time to contrive arguments clever enough to change her mother's plans. Isabel was no help whatsoever. How often had her cousin voiced her eagerness to visit London? Neither Aunt Letitia nor Isabel would be Caroline's ally in the upcoming debate.

As Caroline reached the ground floor, Becky grabbed her hand and dragged her through the bustling kitchen and into the garden. "I think the puppies might be opening their eyes."

"They are only three days old. Perhaps in a few more days."

Rusty, a favorite spaniel of the whole family and mother of many fine hunting dogs for the neighborhood gentry, had made her bed in a crate lined with old blankets in a quiet corner of the garden shed. The dim light and the air, pungent with the scents of lavender and herbs hanging in dried bunches from the rafters, combined to create an enchanted spot.

Rusty perked up her ears as they approached.

"Only five puppies this time." Becky peeked into the crate. "Two brown ones and I think the others are black."

Caroline fondled Rusty's ears. "She has been a fine mother to all her litters. I heard one of the puppies we gave to Mrs. Mersey has a litter of her own. You have founded quite a dynasty, my pretty girl."

Becky counted on her fingers. "I think I can count six now. Maybe Henry missed one."

"What did I miss?" Henry came into the shed.

"Maybe you just cannot count. I can see six puppies." Becky's voice carried a teasing tone.

Captain Ogden entered behind Henry. "My policy is, with kittens and puppies, why even try to count them? Sooner or later they'll introduce themselves, don't you know?"

Becky giggled, and Henry nodded, his self-esteem protected. Caroline kept her eyes on the dogs, all too aware of the handsome rogue standing beside her. What a nuisance to have him here at Sunnyslope when she needed to think, to prepare justifications for postponing the Season. She wanted a clear head, careful reasoning. This afternoon's embarrassment was nothing compared to her real predicament.

She glanced at him, and their eyes met for an instant. In spite of herself, she wondered if he approved of her appearance. Not that she truly cared. Thomas Odgen had nothing to do with the considerable time she had spent choosing the rose-sprigged muslin dress she wore. No, nothing to do with Thomas Ogden. Why did his approval even enter her mind? What a muddle!

She reached down again to smooth Rusty's satiny head. Thomas touched her hand and they both drew back abruptly, recoiling as if handling a burning ember. Her eyes met his once more.

"Permit me, Miss Parker?" He reached for one of the puppies.

She could not look away. Framed by dark lashes, his eyes of gray-green gleamed with an enigmatic glow in the faint light. She stood almost frozen for a moment before breaking the spell and looking away.

Thomas gently put the puppy in Becky's eager hands. "Mama will not mind if you treat her little ones carefully."

Thomas lifted another soft, warm ball of fur and placed it in Caroline's hands. Again their fingers brushed and his lingered, caressing the puppy's tiny silken head and grazing her wrist with his thumb. She watched his hand, large yet gentle, as he petted the tiny dog. Somehow she felt short of breath, strangely unsettled by his presence.

Caroline peeked at Thomas Ogden from beneath her lashes. What a good thing he would take his leave early the next morning. His nearness caused a funny feeling inside her — a sparkly tingle. Her skin felt warm and flushed.

Whatever could be the matter with her? This was not the sensibility needed to engender solutions for her dilemma.

She brought herself back to reality. "We must go in to dinner soon, Captain Ogden. Aunt Letitia will be sending Plummer for us any minute. Becky and Henry, Miss Saverfield will be looking for you two."

She replaced the puppy beside Rusty and watched as Becky did the same and followed Henry toward the nursery. Captain Ogden made a little bow, offering his arm to Caroline. She pretended not to notice the gesture. After lingering beside Rusty for another few moments, she gave Captain Ogden a polite nod, then led the way into the house. With every step, she felt Thomas's eyes on her back and she shivered a bit, though not from the coolness of the temperature.

As Caroline and Thomas joined the others in the drawing room, a footman passed a tray of sherry glasses. Fearing her cheeks still flamed, she stood far from the fire, yet near enough to listen.

Thomas joined Simon and Ned in conversation with Lord Barstow. Naturally, the gentlemen talked of bloodstock.

"I am partial to fine conformation and a well-turned leg." Thomas looked blandly in Caroline's direction.

Caroline did not even blink, ignoring the inference the others would not understand. How dare he provoke her? He certainly was no gentleman despite his town bronze. So why was she conscious of every move he made? She caught herself clenching and unclenching her hands and quickly hid them behind her back.

When Aunt Letitia entered, Captain Ogden bowed to her. "Your children are most charming, Lady Barstow."

Letitia preened at the compliment and Isabel hung on his every word.

"Young Master Henry and Miss Becky are bright and lively young persons. You are fortunate in your entire family."

Caroline could not help smiling at her aunt's obviously astonished twitter.

Lord Barstow drew the discourse back to horses. Ned took the opportunity to praise his pair of blacks, but no one mentioned this morning's caper, to Caroline's relief.

"I take it you've been breeding for speed, sir?" Thomas directed his question to the earl.

"Yes, the stud is thriving, with the off-spring of Thunderbolt having done so well at Newmarket and the Downs, too."

When the butler appeared in the door to announce dinner, Captain Ogden offered Lady Barstow his arm. The others followed them into the dining room.

Throughout the meal the talk remained on horses, but Caroline avoided entering the discussion, pretending she never knew Thomas Ogden smiled at her from time to time. Her discomfort, she told herself, originated from the prospect of a London Season, not from his most vexing attention. With her whole life spinning inside out, how could she fuss so about the first handsome young man she had encountered in ages?

As soon as Aunt Letitia led Isabel and her from the table, Caroline excused herself to go to her room. Her thoughts churned wildly from dilemma to impasse. The tone of her mother's letter was insistently final. Could she talk her mother out of her plans? A strong will belied Lady Clarissa's fragile appearance. No amount of pleading or tears had convinced her to take Caroline back to Stockholm last year. Once they had been so close, a mother and daughter who shared everything. Now it seemed they would be completely at odds.

Caroline set her single candle on the dressing table and sank onto the window seat. Not even her view of Sunnyslope's moonlit park soothed her mind. Years ago she had been like a princess, pampered by her mother and indulged by her father. Had it been in Vienna — or perhaps Madrid — where she had accompanied her mother in the royal gardens, admired by a throng of diplomats and their ladies as they strolled among the manicured flowerbeds? How her childish curtsy was applauded. She fancied nothing more than to imitate the perfect grace and refinement of her adored mother. The two of them had collected lavish compliments from everyone they met, aristocracy and shopkeepers alike.

Now, only a few years later, Caroline knew she had changed. That world seemed far away in every respect. She was not even sure she could execute much more than the most cursory dip without losing her balance. Not that change had come easily, she thought. When her parents decided to leave her at Sunnyslope to experience, as they termed it, an English girlhood, Caroline had just celebrated her tenth birthday. Nothing in her sweetly decorous life to that time prepared her for the boisterous household of her uncle's estate.

Looking back, Caroline hardly believed the misery of those first weeks at Sunnyslope. Ned and Isabel teased, even tortured her. They left her alone in the woods or jumped whooping off balconies when she tried to hide in the shrubbery. Her constant tears incited them to more pranks.

Only in the company of her pony could she find comfort for many forlorn months. Slowly she had changed, learned to give as well as she got. Once as she wandered through a shed near the stables, staying out of sight, she spied a pile of old netting. The next day when cousin Ned hustled into the stables, she dropped it on him from the rafters. Tangled beyond escape, he howled until every nearby stable hand and half the farm staff as well arrived to help. From then on, Caroline and Ned enjoyed a truce, broken now and then by affectionate and harmless pranks.

She and Isabel once shared a hapless lady tutor who was no more adept than their governess at keeping track of two girls who would rather be anywhere but the schoolroom. Once they discovered the tutor's secret cache of Minerva Press novels, however, they tolerated an occasional lesson in exchange for her latest acquisition.

Never, not once in her short lifetime, had she given any thought to her future. And now it might be too late. Perhaps if her mother compromised on the need for finding a husband this year, Caroline could agree to a come out — but only as a last resort. Better if she could talk her mother out of the Season, too. Next year or the year after would be so much better, when she and Isabel could be presented together.

From what she heard, a young lady waited for a gentleman to take the initiative. At every ball, every reception, she would be on display, trying to smile while she just stood and waited for someone to ask her to dance or to make conversation. How thoroughly repugnant! She would have no control at all.

Most of the men would probably be like Thomas Ogden, with his condescending remarks. And to think he had caught her wearing livery. Before dinner, when they were with the puppies, his attitude was entirely too familiar. Why, tonight at the table, she felt too mortified to meet his eye. Being one of those London rakes, he might retell the tale of the ponies. And might even exaggerate, as Ned was wont to do when he talked of his exploits in the city. Not even half of Ned's stories sounded plausible.

Her heart fell to her toes. Odious Thomas Ogden in his London clubs telling the story of her escapade! She could picture herself standing alone at some rout, without a dancing partner, while across the way, a group of simpering dandies passed the story from one to another, laughing at her right out loud. Good heavens, think how Ned had bragged about the Ogden brothers being from a fine old family. And she had been cavorting in white stockings and tight breeches, legs revealed for his leers. Could he ruin her with just a few words? Would she be dragged to London only to become the object of sniggering gossips and stiff-rumped tattlemongers?

The next morning, Caroline went to the stables before breakfast. "Good morning, Will." Her voice was brisk and determined. "I shall take Oberon and Titania out first." The familiar warmth, hay and horse smells, the rustle of eager mounts looking for a treat did not cause her to linger as usual. Already she could see Thomas Ogden's horse being led out of a stall.

Oberon shook his head, jingling his bit, and stamped his shiny black hooves in anticipation. Titania reached her velvety muzzle toward Caroline's hand, knowing that a treat awaited. She fed each pony a carrot, combed their forelocks, and wiped down their necks with a soft cloth. Their already shining coats took on a special sheen, and Caroline admired their burnished smoothness, even as she looked at her hands in displeasure. Her mother would be appalled, she thought, as she belatedly drew on her gloves.

She knew her dark blue riding habit looked suitable, though not exactly correct for driving. Her velvet bonnet hardly reflected the latest style, and the edges of her jacket looked a bit threadbare up close. She had no time to change, even if she had something better. Yet perhaps Captain Ogden might remember her as something of a young lady instead of the hoydenish rattlepate that she had appeared yesterday.

Last night, though Caroline had fretted until well after midnight, she deduced no means of dealing with the likes of Thomas Ogden except directly, in as straightforward a manner as she could, given his distressing propensity to make her uncomfortable. Whatever happened this morning, she intended to behave with dignity and composure.

A touch of frost grazed the paddocks, but the sun peeked through a thin layer of winter clouds. She climbed onto the seat of the small curricle and spread a rug over her lap.

Another dark thought struck her: if she went to London, the ponies would miss their daily workouts and waste all this careful training. But she could just imagine Aunt Augusta's reaction to that argument for postponing her come out.

Setting them off at a smart walk, Caroline headed the ponies down the long driveway. At the gatehouse, she could smell the aroma of bacon, and her stomach gave a little rumble. She waved to Mrs. Beecham, scattering crumbs to a few hens, then turned the rig back toward the house.

Halfway up the long winding driveway, she rounded a curve and saw Thomas Ogden on horseback heading her way. He sat the bay well, obviously at home in the saddle. A chilly breeze ruffled the many capes of his greatcoat. She took a deep breath and straightened her shoulders.

Reining up as he came alongside the curricle, he doffed his hat and smiled. "Good day, Miss Parker. Lovely morning."

There was that disconcerting look again. Why did it make him so handsome instead of merely devilish, she wondered. "And good day to you, Captain Ogden. You have fortunate weather for your journey."

"Yes, indeed. The roads can be quite treacherous this time of year, but today will be fine. Your team looks all the crack this early hour."

"How very kind of you to notice." She smiled, genuinely pleased, if dismayed at the way her heart pounded.

"I am returning in a week or so, Miss Parker, and when I do, I should enjoy discussing your ponies. I admire them very much."

"Again, I thank you for your kind words, Captain Ogden." Perhaps he might not be such a rogue after all.

"Fine ponies are often harder to acquire than horses, I surmise."

"Yes, I have found it so."

"And, Miss Parker, if I may be so presumptuous, you are looking very much in the pink, too, this morning."

"As opposed to my improper attire yesterday, I assume?"

"You looked, ah, shall I say charming?"

She plunged ahead with the question that had been tickling her all night. "Perhaps you could tell me what the *ton* would think of a young lady who drives a curricle in breeches, Captain Ogden."

He did not repress his grin. "I cannot presume to answer for all, but among the elder generation, particularly the females, it would not be admired. In fact, it would put them in mind of another Caro who cavorts in male dress, a poor example for such as you," he added.

"And would such a story be likely to circulate widely?"

"Oh, indeed, it would be a treasured *on dit* — if, that is, such a story was bandied about."

"I may be in London this Season. If this little story remains untold, I would be in your debt, sir."

"Ah, the Season. I am sure you shall truly be a toast, Miss Parker."

She frowned. "My role sounds more like being a filly at auction."

"An apt analogy."

"You have been through Seasons, Captain Ogden. Did you get to know any of the young ladies very well?"

"Hardly. The information is faulty, at best. When buying a filly, one can examine her legs, appraise the depth of her chest, and try her out." He simulated a stiff bow and spoke in an extremely affected manner. "Charmed, Miss Parker, to make your acquaintance. In lieu of inspectin' your teeth or slappin' your rump, would you honor me with this set so that I may test your soundness and try for a glimpse of your ankles?"

Caroline gasped, then broke into laughter in spite of herself. "Well, sir, if I encounter such a partner, I shall truly endeavor to connect his ankle with my foot!"

"Monstrous!" he exclaimed.

"If you honor my plea for your silence, perhaps I shall be able, in some small way, to return your kindness someday."

"Perhaps, Miss Parker." He raised his eyebrows and nodded again. "That is, if the original gesture is made. I shall think it over while I travel." With a wide grin, he waved and touched his heels to his horse, taking off at a swift canter.

Caroline's stomach was tied in knots. He had not exactly promised. Was she in worse shape than before, now beholden to him and vulnerable to his whim? Then again, if the story did circulate and people were shocked, maybe she would not have to go through with the Season this year after all. With that thought as a slight comfort, she started her routine with the team.

A good thing she had a regular route, Caroline thought as she drove the team back into the stable yard an hour later. She still felt all aflutter, unable to concentrate on either the ponies or her own dilemma.

Ned strolled out of the stables and gave her a hand down from the curricle. "Cousin dear, your pair of ponies is bang up to the mark."

"Only because of my superior training techniques. Just wait until you see how I have them set up for a four-in-hand rig."

"Don't gammon me. Not really?" He could not hide his interest. "A pair of ponies ain't so special, but a four-in-hand? That would be unique indeed."

"Yes, we are working hard. Another week or two and I will stand them against any foursome." Of course, where Ned was concerned, she always exaggerated.

"I will be happy to see it." Ned's voice had a mischievous lilt. "And by the way, you'd better watch your flank. After your romp yesterday with these two nags, I owe you one. Remember, I always repay my debts."

Three

As he rode toward Pemstead, Thomas tried to keep his thoughts away from the upcoming visit to his mother. Indeed, he found himself reflecting upon Miss Caroline Parker and her future. Last night he noticed she wore a gown more notable for its simplicity than its stylishness. The candles brought out the golden highlights in her hair, and her delicate beauty made it difficult to believe she had been the author of the morning's prank. No one had explained her presence, but she appeared to be a permanent resident of the estate. Perhaps she was the poor cousin living off the largesse of relatives. He felt a pang of sympathy.

Thomas's half brother, Lionel, had inherited his viscountcy from his mother's first husband. Thomas and Simon were the sons of her second husband, a good man with only a modest income. The family's life of relative splendor was due to Lionel's position and their mother's portion. The brothers had a wonderful childhood at Pemstead in blissful if impish ignorance of the world beyond their neighborhood. But Thomas had been twelve and Simon even younger when their father's death left Lady Elizabeth a widow for the second time.

A chill wind blew at his back as he reined up at the gates to Pemstead, Lionel's estate. The weak winter sun was low in the sky, bringing a silvery glow to the bare trees. How tempting to postpone the meeting with his mother by spending a few hours at the main house with Viscount Pemstead.

How cowardly! No use prevaricating. No use dawdling or conjuring up excuses. Why postpone the inevitable? He rode on toward the village, where the dower house stood at the western edge of the estate.

After Mr. Ogden's death, Lady Elizabeth's mourning period had lasted longer than usual, Thomas recalled. But now, after almost fifteen years, he wondered how content she was to attend her grandchildren, involve herself in village affairs, and work in her garden. He'd never thought of her as particularly meddlesome, but this summons had ominous overtones. If Lady Elizabeth was keeping tabs on his London activities via correspondence, no telling what distortions had been added.

Compared to some fellows with many

years on the town, Thomas considered himself pretty tame, confining his wagers strictly to cards. A few dalliances with lightskirts or opera dancers, perhaps, but not even a hint of an alliance with a married lady, even in the face of numerous opportunities and several outright invitations. But if he was trying to build a case for his own defense, these were negative arguments at best.

Mrs. Broadbent bustled to open the door for him and take his coat and hat. A family retainer at the estate as long as he could remember, Mrs. Broadbent now watched over his mother.

"Her ladyship is in 'er sitting room, Mr. Thomas," she said with a big smile. "I'll git Jake to see to yer horse."

"Thank you, Mrs. B." He patted her shoulder.

Thomas stopped at the upper hall mirror to smooth his dark curls and straighten his cravat, feeling as though he was about to face the executioner.

Lady Elizabeth looked charming, framed as she was at her desk before the oriel window overlooking her garden. With the waning light behind her, she looked about twenty again, an impression she no doubt had planned carefully for maximum effect.

Her hair bore only a few traces of gray; her carriage betrayed nothing of her fifty-some years.

And instead of the stern look he expected, she was smiling.

"Darling Thomas, I have some news of great import, but you must promise not to breathe a word of it to anyone, including your brothers."

Thomas kissed her cheek, genuinely puzzled. Where were the admonishments, the chastising words he expected? The reproaches, the reprimands? "Of course, Mother. I shall keep your counsel."

"Shall I ring for tea? Or would you have spirits?"

"Tea later, thank you. My curiosity is thoroughly piqued."

"And I am bursting to tell you."

She walked to a locked box atop a gilt side table and took out a letter. "Do you remember your father's second cousin George Whitmore?"

Thomas shook his head. Sometimes it seemed there were scores of relatives all over the kingdom.

"You do know your great-great-grandfather was Malcolm, Marquess of Aldonhurst, adviser to the first King George?"

This time he nodded.

"Frederick, the present marquess, is a distant connection of yours. I have not seen him for more than fifteen years. George Whitmore was the heir. I say 'was' because he seems to have succumbed to a fever some months ago, though I never heard a word about it. His wife would have been a poor excuse for a marchioness anyway — a pudding-faced woman with no consequence whatsoever."

She could not hide a smile of pleasure. "But I digress. Apparently most of the children born into the family branches over the generations disappeared into the colonies or died or have been of the female persuasion. Which leaves you as Malcolm's closest direct male descendent."

Thomas was stunned. He could not remember hearing about Aldonhurst, except as some story about an ancestor of his father's who had been at Court long ago.

"To come to the point, my dear son, you will be the next Marquess of Aldonhurst."

A thousand questions burned in Thomas's head, each one more important than the last, as he fumbled to find the chair behind him. But his mother went on before he could find any words at all.

"Frederick is old, over eighty, I presume.

I have tried to make discreet inquiries, but have learned only a little from my friend Dorothea Dunlop who lives near Dunster."

"Where is Aldonhurst?"

"In Somersetshire, though the exact location of the estate I could not say. Fredcrick has been a recluse for some years. Dorothea says he is rather a scholar. Racketed around Greece and Italy. Even wrote treatises on the Roman conquest of Britain."

"I am not sure I understand. I may be the heir to a title and unknown property in a location we cannot precisely identify?"

"Do not be an impertinent slowtop, Thomas!" Lady Elizabeth declared, frowning. "You are a direct descendent of the second marquess, or is it the third? This is a great opportunity for you. Here, my dear, read Frederick's letter. He wants you to come to him."

Thomas read quickly through Aldonhurst's letter. It was nothing more than an invitation to visit, written in the very shaky script of an elderly hand.

Lady Elizabeth watched him anxiously. "What do you think?"

"I have no idea what to think. I've been trained as a soldier. I cannot pretend to know much about running an estate."

His mother gave an exasperated sigh. "I know that the mothers of young ladies find their arrangements very difficult, but I believe that a mother of sons has even more difficult problems. Naturally Lionel is well settled at Pemstead. Those cherubs he and Margaret produced are quite admirable children.

"I worry about you and Simon. What will become of you? Of course Simon, if he cares to be, is exceedingly clever at his studies."

"And I was not?" He grinned and patted her hand. "No, no, I quite agree, Mother. If I had not had the misfortune of meeting up with a French saber, I would have been still sloshing through the Pyrenees chasing that infernal Corsican. Bookwork has never been my forte. But I doubt land management is, either."

"You lived most of your life here at Pemstead. Certainly you have a feel for the land. Anyway, a good bailiff is always required, whether one knows anything or not.

"There is something more," Lady Elizabeth continued. "Dorothea says Lord Aldonhurst seems to be sadly impoverished. Aldonhurst is deplorably run down, and the marquess is quite mad."

She smiled benignly at him. "But I have a plan for restoring the estate and thoroughly ensuring your future. Now, dear, please ring for tea. You must be parched after such a long ride."

Thomas followed his mother's instruction, then settled down on the settee, nodding for her to continue.

"I do know the local gossip says Frederick wishes his successor to take seriously what he himself has disregarded all these years: the establishment of a succession. The land, the property, and the title will go to your heirs."

Thomas could not see the advantage of any title if the estate lay in ruin. But Lady Elizabeth waved him to silence.

"I can think of at least three reasons why you must find yourself a wife. First, the marquess wishes it. Second, you'll need a woman who can run a household when you take over the estate. And third, you need money."

"You expect me to marry for money, Mother? How crass. How deplorable."

"How practical!" she snapped. "There are many young women these days who have their own means, even fortunes. You may as well develop a *tendre* for one of them as for some penniless chit, is that not so?"

"Do you mean to tell me that you are willing to accept a daughter-in-law of less than the highest social standing? Or one that is cross-eyed or awkward or even ugly? Or, God forbid, has ancestors in commerce?"

"Thomas, you do go on so. You know what I mean. Many a perfectly acceptable young lady simply does not take. Perhaps she is shy, or her mama is overbearing. Even the most awkward of girls can turn out to be a social butterfly after several Seasons. The trick is to find one with breeding, money, and potential."

Thomas could not restrain his laughter any longer. "I can hardly believe my ears."

"Thomas!" Her voice was indignant.

Mrs. Broadbent entered and set the tray before Lady Elizabeth.

When Thomas had his cup of tea and she sipped daintily from her own, Lady Elizabeth continued. "There is no shortage of young ladies these days. I will go to London myself to set you up for the Season. Lionel and his wife are not going. We shall have Pemstead House in Hanover Square. I have not been there for several years."

"I think you are looking forward to it."

"Perhaps I am. I will see many old friends. But it will be best if we keep this coming title from the *ton*."

"Yes," he agreed, "since we hardly know what it is all about."

"We will know more as soon as you go to the marquess, but confirming the descent could take months. Sooner or later, the news will leak out. But in the meantime, you will save yourself from gaggles of conspiring mamas."

"My God, do not let anyone know. I cannot imagine being so attacked!"

"Do not exaggerate, dear. But as Captain Ogden you will be able to have a much clearer opportunity to find the most suitable alliance. Although, if the potential of so exalted a title is needed to secure an arrangement . . ."

"Mother!" Thomas exclaimed. "I am astonished . . ."

"Simply leave it all to me."

Later, as he drank a glass of port after dinner, Thomas thought back to his mother's words. Did he have any feeling for land? He never really thought about it before. The idea of owning any property had been much too remote. The poverty of the estate brought the dilemma. Without capital, he could not finance refurbishment of house, home farm, or tenant facilities. The blunt gained from gambling would never be enough, and his luck might change at any moment. Worse yet was the thought of finding a wife, someone he would have to see every day for a lifetime. The future, which he had been regarding with cavalier aimlessness and a complete lack of aspirations, now looked very different indeed.

Aunt Letitia's melancholy moan from the hall alerted Caroline to the imminent arrival of not only Lady Clarissa Parker, but also her sister, Lady Augusta Stolper. Only two days had passed since Caroline had learned of her mother's plan.

"Bring my vinaigrette down, please," Aunt Letitia called to a maid as she bustled down the stairs.

Caroline followed her aunt. She could hardly wait to see her mama, to welcome her back and, more urgently, to plead the case for postponing her come out. As for the idea of imminent marriage, Caroline prayed that had been only a flight of her mother's fancy.

The moment Lady Clarissa stepped over the threshold, Caroline flew around her aunt and into her mother's arms. Mother and daughter were practically a matched pair, with honey blond hair and sparkling blue eyes, now filmed with tears of happiness. Petite and slender, Clarissa at thirty-eight looked more like Caroline's sister than her darling mother.

Caroline's throat tightened and tears spilled down her cheeks. The seven long months since they had been together seemed an eternity. Dressed in a pelisse of deep blue velvet with matching bonnet, Lady Clarissa held her daughter close. For the moment, Caroline forgot everything but her joy.

"My darling," Clarissa murmured. "You have become a young lady now." The tightness in Caroline's throat prevented her response, but she clung tightly to her mother.

Letitia's eyes were moist, her hankie clutched to her bosom as she watched Clarissa embrace Caroline.

In contrast to the tender reconciliation scene, Lady Augusta Stolper presented a stern countenance, matching the dull brown of her traveling ensemble. Her imposing bulk appeared as formidable as an old castle's barbican. Her voice matched her scowl. "Good day, Letitia."

"Good morning, Augusta," Letitia mumbled. "I am glad you came along."

"If I waited for an invitation, I should never see my old home. Where is Jeremy? The trees along the drive need pruning." Without an answer to her question, Augusta swept off in search of her brother, leaving the footmen to dispose of the baggage.

Drying her eyes, Caroline whispered to her mother, "Mama, we must talk. You see, I cannot . . ."

"Of course, we will have a lovely coze as soon as I get settled, my darling. I know you have many questions, and I promise you, everything will be for the best."

An hour later, the party was finally seated at luncheon. Augusta surveyed the table. "Where is Ned?" she asked. "I was under the impression that he had been sent down from Oxford and is now at home."

"Now, Augusta," Lord Barstow began, "the lad don't have a scholarly bent. Does better at home. He has a friend here and they have gone off to the village. He could not know you would be arriving . . ."

"If he had, he would no doubt have been off to a more remote destination." Aunt Augusta's lips were twisted into a tight bow.

Caroline exchanged a glance with Isabel and had to suppress her giggles. Aunt Augusta was all too correct.

"I will have a few words with my nephew upon his return, but for the time being, we should get right to the purpose of our visit." Augusta took a small white card from her sleeve and read a list of activities. "Proper deportment is most important, so we will begin with posture, Caroline. And, Isabel, I can see from your unladylike slump at this very table that you are in need of the same guidance."

This time Caroline looked at Isabel with dismay. She sat a little taller, back straighter, and her cousin followed suit.

Augusta went on. "This afternoon I will hear your performance on the pianoforte and this evening we will begin dancing instruction. As to your complexion and hair, my maid Ellis is an expert. And tomorrow morning, first thing, we will peruse your wardrobe to see if there is anything on hand that will be of use." She turned to her brother. "I am not without an appreciation for the necessities of thrift."

The earl merely nodded, looking entirely helpless.

"Mama," Caroline began, "I am so anxious to show you my team of ponies. They are simply smashing . . ."

"Caroline," Augusta broke in. "The dining room is no place for young ladies to discuss cattle."

"We shall talk later, dear," Clarissa whispered.

Caroline felt like dumping her soup over Aunt Augusta's tight braids. But if she thought her aunt had been severe at the table, Caroline soon learned luncheon was just an initiation to the tone of Augusta's sharp tongue. Immediately upon leaving the table, Clarissa, Isabel, and Caroline were herded into the music room, where Ellis, a personage whose severity of expression surpassed even that of her mistress, awaited. The maid placed books on Caroline's and Isabel's heads and stood like a military drill leader as she marched them around and around the room.

Augusta and Clarissa sat down and watched the parade.

"I cannot imagine what you were thinking of, Clarissa, leaving your daughter here. She should have been with me. I blame myself for not insisting. I could have had her well-prepared, and there would have been none of this hoydenish behavior with animals."

"But when I asked you," Clarissa began,

then paused, apparently finding the rearrangement of her skirts more imperative than finishing her thought.

Augusta went on. "This establishment is poorly run, in my opinion, and too free by far. Our brother should be ashamed to rusticate and let his wife lollygag so. The children need proper supervision. In fact, I view it as a matter of family honor. Young Ned will be the earl, the head of the family someday. And from what I hear, his friends strive to emulate that raffish crowd around the Prince of Wales. They should be developing their abilities to assume responsibility for their families and, indeed, their nation. I am sure I shall have the opportunity to tell Jeremy exactly that. And Ned, too. As for Letitia, her behavior this very afternoon is a perfect example. Imagine pleading the headache before even leaving the luncheon table. What kind of standard is that for the children and the servants? If the countess will not live up to her obligations, then I will have to do so, much as I dislike meddling in the affairs of others."

Caroline lost her balance at this remark and the book on her head crashed to the floor.

"Caroline, keep your back straight. If

you cannot walk properly, how do you think you will look on the dance floor?"

"Yes, Aunt Augusta." When, oh when, Caroline wondered, could she be alone with her mother? When could she get this nonsensical situation straightened out?

Aunt Augusta rattled on and on as if neither Caroline nor Isabel possessed operational ears. "Neither of these young chits has a bit of grace about them. Just look at those red hands. And the mops of hair escaping from those straggling ribbons."

Aunt Augusta's disapprobation deepened when Caroline stumbled through a halting version of *Greensleeves* on the pianoforte.

"Enough!" Augusta demanded.

"The music teacher has not come for a while," Caroline admitted, hoping she would not have to reveal that "a while" meant at least two years.

"I shall send for him this afternoon, so you may expect to spend considerable time at the keyboard, young lady. You will learn at least four pieces suitable for performing before company. Now fetch me your embroidery basket. Young ladies are known by the fineness of their stitches."

Meekly Caroline handed the whole basket to her aunt. She would not make any excuses for the half-finished sampler or the tangle of silk threads inside. Her aunt would have the proper censure at the tip of her tongue.

But Caroline was totally unprepared for a piercing shriek from Augusta.

"A mouse!" Suddenly, all dignity gone, the affronted matron jumped to her feet, arms flailing the air. The basket dropped from her lap and rolled across the floor, scattering scissors, thimbles, spools, and scraps of cloth everywhere.

Clarissa, too, leaped up, her own work-basket tumbling into the chaos. Isabel screamed and hopped up on a chair, gathering her skirts around her.

Out of the corner of her eye, Caroline recognized a ball of fur rolling across the carpet and grabbed it. Ned's revenge, a mere scrap of rabbit fur, had caught Augusta instead of its intended target!

"It was just a fluff of fur." Caroline squelched a grin.

"It was a mouse," Augusta declared. "It tried to nip me."

Lady Clarissa shook her head. "Perhaps it was just your imagination. Why would a mouse be in Caroline's embroidery?"

Isabel climbed down and shook out her skirts. "We found a whole nest of mice once in an old wool muffler, did we not, Caroline?"

"Oh, please stop!" Augusta's voice once more grew strong. "Nothing would surprise me. Get this mess straightened and ring for tea. And tell Plummer to bring me a drop of sherry as a restorative."

While Caroline changed for dinner that evening, a shout from Ned's room, followed by a loud string of curses, brought a satisfied smile to her lips. Apparently his toe had encountered something deep inside his shoe, exactly where Caroline had returned his property to him, wrapped around a stone to lend it substance.

Late that night, Lady Clarissa sat at her dressing table while her maid, Yvette, brushed her golden hair. In the glow from the candles, the long wavy tresses gleamed. Exactly the way Count Lagerstrom loved to see it, she thought. Dear David, so patient and loving. Soon they could be together always, as they had been the last time she had worn this rose-gold dressing gown. She sighed, remembering the thrill of his caresses.

Was she doing the right thing in trying to settle Caroline this year? Am I too selfish, she wondered, taking the coward's path, telling no one the real reason? She leaned into the gentle strokes of the brush. By next year, Clarissa would be a pariah to Augusta and to all polite Society. And with her own ruin, her daughter would be ostracized, too, with no chance at all for Caroline to make a good match.

Clarissa felt the locket around her neck, the golden bauble that for so long had held the tiny miniature of her late husband, Quentin. Now it held the likeness of Count Lagerstrom. My darling David, she thought. Even so far from him, she felt nearly helpless with desire.

Irony of all ironies, the count was tied to a pitiable invalid, a countess whose youthful slide into madness had left her incapable of thinking or speaking. David cared for her with devotion, subjugating even his wish for children. But in the last few months, he and Clarissa had fallen deeply in love, hiding their feelings from everyone at the Swedish Court and the British embassy. Last month the government had appointed Count Lagerstrom to the Swedish delegation to Vienna, where the European powers had gathered to discuss the future now that Napoléon's conquests had crumbled.

When David begged her to accompany

him, Clarissa tortured herself for days, torn between her responsibilities and her heart's desire. At first she resisted the idea of launching Caroline so suddenly and without a generous dowry. Yet she thought of no other way, and in the end, she could not deny his fervent entreaties. They would go to Vienna and live quietly together. Beyond that, neither Clarissa nor David could think. For her own good, Caroline must be married this year. Clarissa knew her daughter's prospects would be nil when her mother's affair was discovered. Not even her sister Augusta — no, *particularly* not her sister Augusta — would ever understand, much less condone it.

When Caroline slipped in the door, Yvette excused herself and at last mother and daughter were alone. Caroline settled on the floor beside her mother and put her arms around her waist.

"My darling girl." Clarissa struggled to maintain her composure. "I hope you do not mind Augusta's carping. She likes to pretend she is a terrible dragon."

"Oh, Mama, I really do not want to go to London this year. I was so hoping that Isabel and I could do our first Season together in a year or two. Oh, please, say we can." Caroline's face shone with anxious innocence, her voice full of trust.

Clarissa laid her cheek atop her daughter's honey curls. She had to be firm and convincing. If Caroline refused outright, Clarissa knew all her dreams were in vain.

"Caroline, the arrangements are already under way. We are very fortunate that Augusta is going to help us. She is a confidante of one of the patronesses of Almack's. Augusta entertains the highest *ton* both in London and in the country. Her daughters made excellent marriages and themselves enjoy some position in Society."

"I do not know why all that matters."

"Augusta has at her fingertips nearly all the names of eligible gentlemen in London and can cite the size of their fortunes, their titles, their future prospects, their gentlemanly attributes, and even comeliness of their persons."

"But what about next year? Could Aunt Augusta help us then instead?"

"As it is, your cousin Louise will need her to attend her confinement later this summer, and who knows what might take her away from town during the next Season?" Clarissa smoothed her daughter's unruly hair. "And you will be happy once you are settled. You will have security and a home of your own."

"But just because I am being presented, why do I have to marry right away?"

Why, oh God, why is this so difficult? What convincing words could she find? "You are a lovely girl. You are bound to be a toast — an Incomparable."

"Aunt Augusta seems to have a different opinion."

"She wants you to improve upon near perfection, my dear. I will not be satisfied with less myself. If you follow her guidance, you will have many offers of marriage. We will only need to choose among them, I am sure."

"But I do not want to marry. I am happy just the way things are."

Clarissa avoided looking into Caroline's eyes. "Of course you have fears and doubts, my darling. But you will see once you meet some nice gentlemen. Marriage is what gives meaning to a woman's life." She could feel Caroline's doubt in her very breath. "Love will change the way you think about the future." That at least Clarissa knew to be true, oh so very true.

"But how would I know if I love someone? Or if he loves me?"

Clarissa squeezed her daughter's hand

and at last met her gaze. Every word came from her heart. "Love is impossible to define, my dear. True love is deep and abiding, an emotion that builds throughout the years." Suddenly Clarissa could not speak. Her eyes filmed with tears. Would she and David have years or just a few months . . .

After a moment, Clarissa went on. "Of course you want to love your husband, and I am sure you will. But sometimes love comes after marriage and grows through the years."

Caroline shook her head and stared at her hands with such a look of anguish that Clarissa felt her emotions near the breaking point. "You must open your heart, my darling. When you have the opportunity of love, and I promise you will, you will find feelings in yourself that will elevate every sensibility. Soon love will flourish."

"But I do not want to marry someone I do not love." Caroline spoke in a near whisper.

"You must marry someone who wants to care for you and make you his wife. Then love will grow and thrive," Clarissa claimed.

"I am not sure I want to be taken care of."

"Of course you want a man to care for you."

"Why?"

Clarissa chose her words carefully. "A woman has a difficult time without a husband unless she has an ample income."

"I can stay here at Sunnyslope. I do not need to go away, ever. Aunt Letitia said I always have a home here. I can raise my ponies and when they are sold, I shall have an income. You know I already have six ponies and there will be another born soon."

"Be reasonable, my dear. To be the spinster cousin to the family Ned will raise here one day? Do you want to live under the instruction of his future wife?"

"I forgot about him. I shall find another place."

Clarissa lifted Caroline's chin and met her eyes again. "I want you to be happy, Caroline. Perhaps Augusta is right. Having you stay here at Sunnyslope was a mistake."

"Oh, no, I love it here."

"Of course you do, but you have little experience of the world. Now you think I am being unkind and unreasonable by submitting you to Augusta's tutelage, but she knows whereof she speaks. In a few weeks'

73

time, you will forget all your objections, and have to spend every minute deciding which of your beautiful dresses to wear, debating which of the eager gentlemen to honor with your company, taking drives in the park, meeting so many fascinating people, visiting the galleries, dancing at the balls. There now, do not make your poor mother into an ogre for wanting the best for you." At last, Clarissa thought, she had found her voice. "Do not miss out on your beauty sleep, my darling."

When her daughter had gone, Clarissa fell to her knees beside her bed. "Oh, God," she prayed. "Help me do what is best for all of us."

In her room, Caroline sat on her window seat, slumped against the wall. She felt empty, bewildered, and downcast, yet anxious to find refuge in sleep. Dancing and deportment proved to be quite exhausting. She could have worked days in the stables without feeling so tired. But defiance muddled her mind as thoroughly as before. Her mother's explanations and justifications sounded flimsy to Caroline, but talking her out of the Season had been impossible tonight. Nevertheless, Caro promised herself to keep trying.

Just as she prepared to slip under the sheets, Ellis entered the room with a large white jar. Aunt Augusta's maid was not about to let her climb into bed quite yet.

"Guaranteed to improve your complexion and soften your hands, miss," Ellis stated grimly. From her pocket she produced a small bottle of oil, which she soothed onto Caroline's face. In the looking glass Caroline's cheeks shown as glossily as the ponies' brass harness fittings.

Ellis rubbed a sticky concoction of honey and beeswax into Caroline's hands, then covered them with a pair of cotton gloves. "You sleep this way every night, miss, and your hands will be a credit to you."

If she had not heard the words from the dour Ellis herself, Caroline might have believed this routine to be a reprisal designed by her cousin Ned.

Four

Following the directions of a Dunster inn-keeper, Thomas turned down a narrow, overgrown lane, hardly more than a rutted trail, a half-hour's ride from the village. The once proud gates stood wide open and rusty, strangled by brush and a thicket of weeds. Clearly they had not been used in decades.

Rounding a bend, he confronted the façade of a house built of mellow old brick with tall paned windows. Nearly covered with heavy vines, the building had a high roof flanked by symmetrically placed chimneys. The graceful mansion must have dated from the seventeenth century reign of William and Mary. But the closer he got, the more he saw signs of neglect. Clumps of bushes marred the uncut park. Cracked and broken, a fountain stood in the center of the weedy gravel drive.

A gaunt old man with a woolen shawl draped around his shoulders answered the door. The butler was obviously as antique as his master, Thomas thought, as he announced himself.

"Captain Thomas Ogden to see the Marquess of Aldonhurst."

"Come in, my boy. Let's go into my library."

Abruptly, Thomas realized the marquess stood before him and bowed deeply. "Thank you, my lord."

The interior of the house was dim, silent, and chilly. Salons and dining rooms sat hidden behind closed doors. Only the fanlight above the door lit the dark hall. But the cold, empty feeling left Thomas when he entered the bright, south-facing library.

"My old eyes need lots of light." The marquess waved Thomas to a chair.

Thomas looked around the dusty room. Piles of books covered a huge desk in front of the window. More books filled floor to ceiling shelves and lay scattered on two large tables, along with several fragments of Greek or Roman statuary. Though the room was warmer than the hall, the only fire burned low, and the woodbin was almost empty. Near the fireplace a tapestry rug draped a large sofa. The marquess probably slept here, Thomas thought.

As Thomas sat, an old tiger cat hissed.

"Grimalkin is all I have left of a fine kennel of dogs, a stable full of horses and cats, barn cats, house cats, kitchen cats, so many cats that we never saw a mouse in the old days." Aldonhurst's faded blue eyes took in Thomas's dark hair and broad shoulders. "You look like a Whitmore. The family traits are there," he muttered, mostly to himself.

The next few days amazed Thomas as much as they would change the course of his life. Little by little, from the fragments of information the marquess imparted, Thomas heard about the exploits of his distant ancestor, the first marquess who served Charles II in the restoration of the monarchy. He heard about the career at Court of John, the fourth marquess, back in the days of George II. He heard about the retirement of Frederick, the present and sixth marquess, who abhorred the failure of the government to supply the armies in the colonies. He heard about Lord Frederick's devotion to the study of the classics, his years in Greece, Italy, and southern France. And he heard about Lord Frederick's survey of the part of the Roman Fosse Way, the ancient highway that ran through Aldonhurst. All this was interspersed with stories from Suetonius and Tacitus and long silences while the old marquess dozed.

In the latter intervals, Thomas filled the

woodbin and restocked the outer wood-pile. He arranged for a local woman to check on Lord Aldonhurst twice a day and see to his needs. He looked over the land, largely scrub now, with only a few flocks of sheep in the distant rolling hills. He inspected a few tenant houses, found them run-down and home to dispirited folk who looked discontented in the extreme. He found the bailiff, a shifty-eyed man named Silvester, and asked for a full written accounting of the estate affairs, a request Thomas had little expectation of being fulfilled. The arrangements required a large chunk of the remaining blunt from his London gaming.

The night before Thomas intended to leave, the marquess, awakening from a short nap, suddenly asked, "Did you know the Romans were here in England for hundreds of years? About the same amount of time that separates our age from Henry the Fifth and the Battle of Agincourt."

Thomas expressed his surprise at the length of the Roman occupation of England.

The marquess went on in a thoughtful voice. "That makes one realize that a one-hundred-forty-year heritage for Aldon-hurst is not so long after all. I suppose people roamed these hills in the Roman days much as they did in Henry's, and as they do in ours, tending flocks and weaving wool cloth, scratching a living from the soil."

Thomas thought of how little he really knew of history. Only the great battles had held his interest before, not how people lived.

"I am counting on you, my boy, to restore our heritage, sire a family, and ensure the succession. All the things I failed to do." He reached for Thomas's hand. "You will, my boy. Tell me you will."

Thomas took the frail white fingers in his large suntanned hand. "I promise, my lord. I will restore Aldonhurst and secure its future."

"Thank you, Thomas. Thank you . . ." Lord Aldonhurst's voice faded and soon he slept once again. Thomas found himself both deeply touched and frightfully aware that he had given his word. As Lord Aldonhurst had quoted Caesar, "The die is cast."

Caroline set the new hat at a jaunty angle, stared at the result in the cheval glass, then pulled it lower on her forehead and squinted at her reflection. Better.

Feeling quite a la mode, Caroline strode to the stables for her morning workout with the ponies before her mother and her aunt arose. Dawn was the only time she had to herself.

To her surprise, Ned helped the stable boy put the finishing touch on the four-in-hand harness. His hair was tousled and his jacket misbuttoned.

"Why, Ned," she breezed. "You have not been to bed yet?"

"Don't be a goose," he replied. "I got up at this improbable hour to see these improbable nags."

"I do not believe that for a moment."

"You ain't turning into Aunt Augusta, are you?"

"Certainly not. But you have been far too docile. What kind of tricks are you planning? Will my rig tumble into a hidden pit when we head down the lane?"

Ned boosted her into the driver's seat, handed over the reins, and spoke to the ponies. "I declare, your mistress is learning to be as beastly as our nasty aunt."

"If you are riding along, get to it," Caroline said, as she snapped her whip above the ponies' backs.

Ned swung himself aboard and they moved off. "So you are going to snabble

81

yourself a husband in London?"

"Do not pretend it matters a whit to you!"

"It don't. Though I endorse the idea completely."

"The idea of marriage? Why ever would you care?"

"Look at life from my point of view." His voice was suddenly serious. "I am almost twenty-one. I do nothing but father's bidding. I have no responsibilities, none. And he treats me like a child."

"You must admit you occasionally earn that treatment."

"I wish I was the one supposed to make a match. If I married, Father would have to give me a decent allowance and a place to live. I could be independent, have a house of my own. I know Father don't think so, but I could do something with myself besides waiting around for him to . . . to . . ."

"Why do you think he wants you to go back to Oxford?"

"I will never be a scholar. Simon has the knack, but not me. Father knows university is not right for me. He never went, either, but he uses my lack of interest in books as a reason to continue treating me like a child. Why is marriage right for you and not for me? I am three years older than you."

Caroline shook her head, nearly upsetting her hat. "I do not find marriage right for me. Our situations are entirely different."

"Don't you want the independence of your own household?"

"How independent are wives? Everything is under the control of their husbands."

"All I know is that I don't feel like a man. Aunt Augusta is always talking about how I will be head of the family some day. But Father treats me like a child."

Before returning to Sunnyslope, Thomas journeyed in search of the soldier with whom he had shared both his last battle and his early convalescence. The Bristol waterfront tavern resounded with raucous noise, but he found a table in the rear, where the light was dim and the quiet allowed for serious conversation. This detour on his return from Aldonhurst to Sunnyslope was a vital mission.

A shabbily dressed man took the chair opposite Thomas.

"Ev'nin', Cap'n." He propped his crutch against the table. "What brings you to these parts?"

"Seeking you, Joshua."

"Me?"

"How are you getting on?"

"Not too bad." Josh shifted in his chair and played with his cap. "Get some clerking from time to time here at the docks, but a one-legged farmer starts at a disadvantage even here."

After three days spent searching for Joshua Deeble, Thomas confirmed his suspicions. The chief clerk from their old unit did not find civilian life accommodating. How could he, having lost a leg and being thrust back into a world that hardly remembered its far-off war? At Talavera, both the captain and the clerk, mangled by the same cannon shot, were given up for dead. Later, Thomas escaped the surgeon's knife, though whether his reprieve derived from a less severe wound or pure luck he did not know.

"I have a proposal for you. A confidential mission, if you want the job."

"I'm listening, all right, Cap'n!" Josh's voice gave away his eagerness.

"I want you to write down an old man's memoirs." Thomas told Josh all about the Marquess of Aldonhurst and his possible inheritance. "Even if my inheritance goes awry, his history is worth having in the family. But that's not quite all I have in mind. I need a little reconnaissance work

84

as well. The bailiff is undoubtedly cheating the old man and the tenants at the same time. I need to know the extent of the fraud, if anything can be recovered, and how many of the tenants would be worth keeping."

"Might take me a few weeks, but I could do that. No better man to assess the worth of a farmer than one who cannot measure up anymore." Josh gave an ironic chuckle.

"And, Josh, the old marquess is frail. Your highest priority is to see he's taken care of. Equip yourself with a horse and buggy. Tell him I sent you. He's an engaging old fellow. I will pay you for six months, but bring me an interim report in London in three months' time."

Thomas smiled to see the glitter in Josh's eyes replace their former dullness.

The bright blue of the sky lifted Thomas's spirits as he neared Sunnyslope. The bewildering events of the last weeks left him confused, even numbed by the implications of his coming inheritance. The frail old marquess was a charming and colorful character, when he was making any sense at all. But the estate was a ruin. Clearly the bailiff lined his own pockets without producing income for Aldonhurst.

Thomas would have to depend upon his own abilities to return the land to profitability.

Who was he trying to fool? What did he know about crops and livestock?

He rode directly to the stable yard to leave his horse. The two youngest Mortimer children, Becky and Henry, were so involved in their argument they did not notice his arrival.

"Ginger is not a silly name," Becky declared, stamping her foot.

"Sounds like a lapdog," Henry answered.

"Does not."

"Why not Dragonslayer or Sir Galahad?"

Thomas could not help laughing out loud, and when the two children looked up, they ran to his side.

"Come and see the puppies and how they have grown. Papa says we can keep one for ourselves," Becky bubbled. "But we cannot agree on a name." She took Thomas's hand and led him into the stables. "Come and look."

Rusty and her brood had been moved to an empty stall, where the six puppies tumbled over each other in the straw. When Thomas had sufficiently admired the handsome dogs, Henry shook his head and spoke with an air of conspiracy.

"We hide out in the stable most of the time now," he whispered.

"Why is that?" Thomas inquired.

Becky snuggled a puppy in her arms. "Our Aunt Augusta is here, and Caroline's mother, too. They are making Caroline ready for her London come out."

"Aunt Augusta is going to catch her a husband," Henry added.

"Oh, she is?" Thomas responded.

"Yes, Aunt Clarissa — that's her mama — says she must get married right now."

Something about this conversation sounded familiar to Thomas, reminiscent of his own mother's counsel.

Henry went on without a break. "And he has to have a fortune, Aunt Augusta says. Aunt Augusta says that is the best kind of husband."

Becky's voice was almost sorrowful. "Caroline has to learn to curtsy and sing and do all sorts of things, and especially she must look very pretty because she has to find a rich husband. Aunt Augusta says she will have a very hard time. Isabel is going to London, too, but Aunt Augusta says she has to wait until next year or the next for her come out. This year she has to learn everything about being a lady."

Henry took up the tale. "And they are all grumpy! Mama hardly comes out of her bedroom. Yesterday they spread clothes all over the beds. We were hiding behind the drapes and you should have heard Aunt Augusta. She gives orders like a general, Papa says."

"They're going to take apart all the dresses and sew them back together again." Becky clung to one of the puppies. "Aunt Augusta says everything is too old-fashioned. But if you ask me, she's the most old-fashionedest thing I've ever seen."

Henry grinned naughtily. "Aunt Augusta called Caroline a hoyden. Aunt Augusta says Caroline will have no second chances. She has to be very special because she has no money."

"Except," Becky reminded, "Father offered to set her up with a bit of dowry. Aunt Augusta says it is too little to matter, but it was enough to make Mama swoon."

"That's because Mama knows they'll have to have a treasure chest of gold to get anybody to marry you someday!"

"Will not!"

Henry ignored Becky's outburst. "Papa hides from them. Ned and your brother get away whenever they can, but every night they have to help with the dancing lessons."

"Sounds like adequate penance for their past transgressions." Thomas felt compassion for the lovely young Caroline. What a pity that her fresh country charm might be spoiled by what Aunt Augusta said. The so-called hoyden-esque part of her person set her apart and made her delightfully attractive.

Later in the drawing room, as he was introduced to the august Lady Augusta Stolper, Thomas decided that her reputation could hardly be more formidable than her demeanor.

Her lips pursed to match her censorious frown, she acknowledged his introduction with a curt nod. "Captain Ogden, your mama was an acquaintance of mine thirty years ago."

From her expression, Thomas could almost hear her disapproval of Lady Elizabeth's marriage to his father. Lady Augusta was obviously among those who were such good friends when his mother was a viscountess but rarely ever saw her after she married plain Mr. Ogden.

Forcing himself to outdo her dignity,

Thomas simply bowed and said nothing, using the arrival of a footman with a tray of sherry to move away.

Caroline and another young woman entered the room together. Thomas smiled, relieved to see Caroline's innate sparkle was not dimmed by her aunt's instructions. Was he just imagining the challenge in the look she gave him? The impish tilt to her head mischievously repudiated her angelic smile and demure demeanor as she came toward him.

"Mother, this is Captain Ogden, Simon's older brother. Captain Odgen, may I present my mama, Lady Clarissa Parker?"

"Miss Parker, Lady Clarissa, your servant." Thomas made his bow. "I hope it would not be too forward of me to say I expected you to be introduced as Caroline's sister rather than her mother."

With a slight blush, Lady Clarissa smiled and tapped his arm with her fan. "Captain Ogden, I hardly know whether to be flattered or to question the acuity of your eyesight."

Caroline observed the exchange with amusement. "Shh, Mother. Aunt Augusta will admonish you for flirting if you are not careful." Turning to Thomas, she went on. "Aunt Augusta is overseeing my metamorphosis from a cowslip into a rosebud. She says flirting is vulgar and common, most unladylike."

Thomas detected a note of irony in Caroline's voice, but her smile was as sweet as honey.

Lady Clarissa raised one eyebrow, then spoke. "You will have to excuse Caroline, Captain Ogden. Any deficiencies in her behavior are likely to be nothing more than a reaction to my sister's regimen of activities, which keeps my daughter away from training her beloved ponies. Perhaps while you are here Caroline will show you how well behaved they are."

He could not resist teasing her just a little bit. "I was fortunate to have observed a splendid display by Miss Parker's ponies last month."

Caroline tried to shake her head without attracting her mother's attention.

"I found the pair most charming and driven very well, with a degree of finesse I could only call feminine while at the same time she handled them with a skill that was almost masculine."

He smiled directly into Caroline's eyes, now narrowed with anxiety. Her cheeks were flushed and her hands were tightly clenched. No doubt afraid he would tell about her wearing the servant's livery, he thought.

Lady Clarissa beamed, taking his remark as a compliment to her daughter. "I am quite sure your approbation is a welcome bonus to Caroline's pleasure."

The announcement of dinner prevented his further teasing of Caroline. He offered his arm to Lady Clarissa and escorted her to the table.

The tediously proper dinner conversation centered on the weather and the appearance of some sort of bird or other that might or might not foretell an early summer. Thomas, not taking an active part, watched Caroline pointedly ignore him. Her aunt's tutelage had resulted in a more flattering arrangement of her golden curls. The blue of her gown matched the color of her eyes, and its style was entirely becoming. But she would not look his way even for an instant.

Not for the first time, Thomas felt a stab of regret. How unfair that neither of them had means. He had nothing to offer her except a struggle to restore a broken down estate. She lacked the kind of ample fortune that could help him rescue Aldonhurst and maintain her in style until its restoration was accomplished. Of course, she probably would not have been interested in him anyway, but he was quite taken with her. She had beauty and charm and high spirits, perhaps the kind of a female with whom he could spend his lifetime.

Lady Augusta was holding forth on the importance of maintaining an impeccable reputation. "In Society," she intoned, "one's standing is so easily lost. Even the smallest misstep can endanger one's position."

Thomas could not resist the challenge. "Why is this so important, Lady Augusta, when stories race around after one another so quickly that today's prized *on dit* is tomorrow's forgotten item?"

Augusta disregarded the point of his question. "Ladies and gentlemen of quality do not gossip. Topics such as the misconduct of certain prominent persons should never be discussed."

Thomas continued his probe. "If no one discusses misconduct, then how do all the stories streak through the *ton* so swiftly?"

Ned chimed in. "Good point! In fact, Aunt Augusta, at White's, the members even bet on who is, ah, seeing whom."

Lady Augusta could not be deterred from her course. "Propriety is essential in social intercourse. The insidious nature of gossip is an evil that needs to be stamped out," she admonished. "I truly regret that the Prince of Wales's influence on young people today is not more wholesome. But polite society should never discuss his personal life, even though it is less than exemplary."

"If no one mentions his peccadilloes, then how have you heard about them?" Lord Barstow asked.

As Augusta colored and glared at her brother, Caroline dived in. "Reputations appear to be quite fragile."

Lady Clarissa spoke softly. "True, my dear. Being the subject of the wrong kind of discourse can ruin a person."

Caroline shook her head. "Society is unkind and very unforgiving. From what I hear, even the highest of high sticklers are quick to place the worst possible interpretation on the flimsiest of information."

Augusta had recovered her voice. "Spreading such information would be abhorrent, but I fear it is done."

Thomas spoke again. "A true gentleman would never pass on information that would besmirch a lady's reputation, particularly if he held that information in confidence."

"Exactly my point," declared Lady Augusta. "Captain Ogden, you may be a rash young man in some respects, but you have indubitably voiced the essence of my thoughts."

Letitia looked puzzled and turned to Clarissa. "I perceived the essence of her thoughts to be the prevention of tittle-tattle."

Thomas took advantage of a dash of laughter to lean across the table toward Caroline. "The question is," he whispered, "when we are in London, will you find me to be a gentleman?"

When the ladies left the dining table, Lord Barstow led Thomas, Simon, and Ned into the billiard room, followed by a footman with the port. The earl immediately lit his pipe. "This is the only place my sister Augusta will let me smoke. Woman's a pest of the first water. Captain Ogden, I appreciate you and Simon staying here for a few weeks. Gives Ned and me an excuse to avoid . . . well, I hope you know what I mean."

Thomas suppressed his grin. "I believe I do, sir. Simon and I will have more than enough of dancing when we are in London."

"Father, why can I not stay here with you instead of going to London?" Ned asked.

"Nonsense, my boy. You cannot tell me you'd rather loll around this place than go to all the fancy routs and the like."

"Not with Aunt Augusta around. She'll be sure to have her spies tell her the second I darken the door of any place where men have real entertainment."

"Won't hurt you to stay out of those places. You don't have enough allowance to exercise at the tables."

Ned shook his head in exasperation, then took up his billiard stick, joining Simon and Thomas at the table.

After two boisterous games, Thomas slipped out of the billiard room onto the terrace. Lord Barstow had nodded off. Ned and Simon tried to outdo one another at trick shots.

Walking to the balustrade, Thomas welcomed the chilly fresh air. The sky was filled with stars, as bright as they were on nights in Portugal when he so often dreamed of far-off England and its verdant beauty. Now he faced a future that was full of uncertainty. Gazing at those stars, which also watched over his comrades, those who had returned with injuries that left them unable to provide and those left behind in foreign graves, he felt grateful. At least he had his health back, or most of it.

Why be pessimistic? An estate might bring purpose to his life, land and people over which he had responsibility. As for a family, well, the right wife could be an asset, though why the image of Miss Caroline Parker jumped immediately into his head was impossible to discern.

Thomas wondered how Josh was getting along at Aldonhurst. The farmer-clerk's best quality, perhaps, was his instinct about men. Josh could recognize the potential for gallantry in a fellow as quickly as he could detect the one who was not above cheating his mates at cards. Thomas knew Josh's report would be clear and complete.

Thomas sauntered down the terrace, not yet ready to rejoin the carefree antics of his brother and Ned. Through the open doors of the next room, he could hear Caroline's voice. Quickly he drew back into the shadows and looked inside. Caroline stood alone in the center of the music room, turning the pages of a small volume. A frown creased her lovely forehead and her shoulders slumped as though in resignation. She peered at a page for a moment, then spoke aloud. *"Shall I compare thee to a summer's day?"*

"Thou art more lovely and more temperate." Thomas stepped through the half-open door into the music room.

Caroline started in surprise, then smiled. "What do you think of that sonnet? Could I deliver it without making all the older ladies reach for their vinaigrettes?"

"Why are you reciting Shakespeare?"

"Aunt Augusta expects me to perform for her friends. If I have to stand up and declaim, I would rather be Lady Macbeth in the sleepwalking scene, but my good aunt nearly collapsed at the thought. Too bloodthirsty, I suppose."

"Why not the sweet and innocent Juliet?" Thomas asked.

"In my opinion, Juliet is a perfect simp. I decided to try the sonnets, but most of them would shock the old dears, too. Widows and false women's fashion, old age and 'loathsome canker' — my, my what a bumblebroth he wrote about."

"I take it this will be your first Season, Miss Parker."

"I do not look forward to it, but my mother insists."

He noted she made no mention of the

marriage quest Henry and Becky talked about. "I thought only the gentlemen found the Season so daunting and so wearisome. I thought the ladies loved every minute of every fete."

Caroline shook her head and grimaced. "No wonder the gentlemen become bored. Aunt Augusta has me spending hours practicing the pianoforte and trying to sing, if you can imagine. Not to mention learning to smile all over again. 'Very sweetly, not too wide, do not show your teeth. Now laugh as though you were the tinkling of the chimes.'" She demonstrated her newfound ability with more of a simper than a smile and a sound that made her break into genuine laughter. "I think I sound like a donkey."

"Or a peahen in distress!" Thomas joined in her mirth. "Having no sisters, I never realized what preparation for the Season would be like for a young lady. I suppose I concluded you knew about these things merely by the fact of being female. I perceive I am in error."

"Certainly in my case you are, Captain Ogden. But then, you already know the worst about me."

"On the contrary, I know the best about you. You are kind to animals and children;

your skill with cattle is unparalleled; you are a first-class whip. And your looks and charm are quite overpowering. I predict you will do very well in your Season."

"Truly, it is kind of you to say so. Isabel is delighted to be going, but I will miss my ponies more than anything. All the training I have done in the past few months will be wasted."

Thomas could not help smiling at the cloud that suddenly transformed her features. "Why don't you take them along to London?" he asked. "Driving them in the park and in the city streets will be excellent discipline for them." He did not dare add that she might also attract significant attention.

"Do you think I could?" She was suddenly breathless with enthusiasm. "Oh, what a splendid notion, Captain Ogden. I must find Mama right away."

As she rushed out of the room, Thomas stood for a moment. He cursed the impossible situation. As stunning as she was and as promising as his feelings were for her, Caroline Parker did not have a feather to fly with, no more than he himself had. His mother would arrange his introduction to eligible young ladies with considerable dowries that would come to him upon marriage. Feelings, even compatibility, were not a concern.

And Lady Elizabeth was a practical woman. In case her choice was less than enchanting, his mother probably would not be surprised if he took a wife *and* acquired a mistress at roughly the same time. That was, after all, much more common than marrying for love. Whatever love was, he thought with a sigh.

Caroline Parker might be an ideal, but that certainly did not mean he was falling for her. . . .

Five

Caroline arose very early, avoiding new schemes for improvement, too early even for most of the stable boys. The barely risen sun winked through the distant trees, and she shivered in the early morning chill.

In the quiet stables, she kept up a bright flow of endearments to Oberon and Titania, brushing them to a proper sheen, but her thoughts were serious. Last night, before she had a chance to talk to her mother about taking the ponies to London, Aunt Augusta began the dancing lessons.

"How would you like to learn all about the city traffic, my pet?" she asked Oberon as she polished his shiny neck. "Quite a change from our usual routes, if only I can talk to Mama in private. That is the first step, making her agree. But then, my sweet, we have to confront the real predicament."

The pony nuzzled at her shoulder, as if in reassurance.

"How can I convince Mama I do not need to marry? And what can I do with myself once I succeed? If I have no husband and no money of my own, I will just be a burden on somebody. So, what else can I do? A governess needs some accomplishments, and Aunt Augusta says I have none."

She buckled the harness herself, fumbling in her heavy gloves. Her soft, feminine hands pleased Caroline more than she cared to admit. Luckily, the ponies behaved perfectly as she backed them between the curricle shafts. Fastening the straps, she asked, "Why can a lady not be self-reliant, without depending on a man?"

To her surprise, Thomas Ogden offered an answer. "You seem to be doing very well on your own. Good morning, Miss Parker."

"Good morning, Captain Ogden." Caroline suppressed her thought that he had risen unusually early for a self-declared London rake. She thought dandies like him preferred to stay in bed until early afternoon.

"Do you always hitch your team yourself?"

"No, indeed. The stable boys will be here soon. But I want the most time possible with the team. Later, Aunt Augusta has a variety of activities for me — French conversation, elocution lessons, pianoforte practice, and deportment. I would rather deport myself to the billiard room."

"I have heard you have admirable skills at billiards."

"From the tone of your voice, you mean admirable skills for a female, I suppose?"

"I doubt that Aunt Augusta would approve."

"It would be difficult to play the game and hold a fan at the same time."

"Not to mention a teacup."

She laughed and turned to tuck Oberon's forelock under his bridle. She was surprised when the captain held out a piece of carrot for the pony.

"I have been robbing the kitchen garden," he confessed. "Could you tolerate some company on your mission?"

She felt a stab of apprehension. Alone on the narrow seat with Thomas Ogden? She categorized him as a typical London rake. Who knew what he might try? But perhaps she should take advantage of the opportunity to acquire some experience in dealing with such as he.

"I'd be pleased to hear your judgment of the ponies."

Once ensconced in the small curricle with the ponies tossing their heads in the crisp air, Caroline felt his leg firmly pressed against hers. Would not Aunt

Augusta love this, Caroline thought. Not even a groom to chaperon.

Thomas seemed unfazed. "Tell me," he asked, "how did you become involved in training ponies?"

"I wanted to learn to drive. When I first came to live here at Sunnyslope, Uncle Jeremy gave me a pony of my own, a pretty little mare. I found this miniature curricle behind an old wagon when my cousins and I played hide and seek."

"And you taught yourself?"

"In a way I did. I have always loved animals, and horses are my favorite." So saying, she flicked her whip in the air above their backs, the signal to move off at a fast trot.

"Uncle Jeremy thought a female being so involved with horses was not quite proper, but the ponies seemed another story."

"And look how nicely they go now."

"I spent almost every minute with them the first year."

"Where had you lived before?"

"My father was a diplomat, and we lived abroad. Aunt Augusta did not approve of that at all. She said my parents treated me like a pet, but I did not know how other children lived then. When Father was sent to Stockholm, my mother thought I ought to have an English childhood just like hers. So they sent me here."

She guided the pony team onto the track bordering the woods. "I had never lived around other children, and I was really quite afraid of Ned and Isabel. I used to hide in the stables to get away from them." She smiled to herself, remembering her surprise at the cousins' rowdy behavior. "Eventually I became accustomed to having cousins as close as sisters and brothers."

"I have two brothers, but I have never played such a great practical joke as you did on Ned."

"He may never forgive me for making a cake of him in front of you and Simon. If Ned was not already in trouble about Oxford, he might make my London visit unbearable by embarrassing me at every opportunity. Or do you plan to take over that duty for him?"

"You might be surprised at what I have in mind."

She pulled the ponies to a stop and a mischievous gleam showed in her eyes. "Give me your word of honor you will behave, Captain Ogden, or else I shall make you walk back to the house and ruin your boots." She looked down at his highly polished Hessians.

He laughed. "Miss Parker, if you make me walk that far without my stick, not only the boots will be ruined. I'd have to take to a Bath chair rather than lead you out in London."

Caroline's thoughtlessness left her chagrined and ashamed of herself. "Oh, I am so sorry, I did not mean to . . ."

"Think nothing of it. Lucky for me that the one thing a gentleman hardly ever has to do is walk any distance at all." He placed his hand over hers and grinned. "Perhaps I should thank the Frenchies for saving me from a heartless miss with no regard for a man's boots."

Even through her glove, the heat of his hand sent a stirring sensation up her arm. But instead of making her warmer, she shivered.

"Are you cold?" he asked, moving his arm around her shoulder.

"A bit," she lied, feeling strangely short of breath. For just a second she let the feeling wash over her, then shifted a little away from him on the seat. "Really, I am fine. But we should get moving again." She clucked to the ponies, and their harness began to jingle once more as they picked up their fleet pace.

"Rest assured, Miss Parker, it will not be

my purpose to humiliate you before the *ton*, not at all. Though I insist on reserving the right to tease you in private, and I may require the occasional honor of your presence on the dance floor."

"You really are planning to spend the Season in London?" Caroline asked.

"Yes, my mother is returning for the first time in several years and I have promised to attend her from time to time. I am certain our paths will cross frequently."

Later in the morning, Caroline finally contrived to get her mother alone for the purpose of strolling in the garden. Aunt Augusta's never-ending correspondence granted a welcome reprieve from lessons before luncheon.

Caroline linked her arm through Lady Clarissa's. "Mama, I know you are disappointed that I am reluctant to go to London. I have an idea that will make it easier for me."

"What is that, my dear?"

"Let me take the four ponies along."

Clarissa stopped and looked at her daughter in surprise.

Caroline rushed on. "I will be able to continue training them by driving in the park. It will even be good for them to learn town as well as country manners."

"But what will Augusta think of that?"

Caroline stifled an urge to ask who cared. "Why would it matter to her? I will go to the park early in the morning and the rest of the day I will be in good spirits. I promise."

Caroline could feel her mother weakening.

"We would have to take a groom along." Lady Clarissa looked thoughtful.

Caroline envisioned imminent victory. "Yes, and he could help with Uncle Barnaby's horses, as well. Just yesterday Aunt Augusta was wondering how their grooms could cope with all the extra horses. The ponies would not be much trouble at all."

"Well, I am not so certain of that. But I will consult with Augusta and perhaps we can work something out."

That very afternoon, Caroline triumphed. As the four ladies sat to stitch, Lady Clarissa smiled at her daughter. "You will need more carriage dresses, Caroline, if you are to be driving in the park every day."

Disapproval was etched in Augusta's frown, but she did not contradict her sister.

Caroline could hardly suppress her most unladylike urge to jump for joy, but she contented herself with a big squeeze for her mother. "You will not regret your generosity, Mama."

Augusta's voice carried a tone of warning. "You must be very careful that you do not become an object of discussion in the wrong places, Caroline. I cannot say I approve of taking those animals along, but if we can thus prevent continual sulks, I reluctantly agree."

Caroline gave immediate evidence of her spirit of cooperation by sewing a very decorative row of tiny tucks alternating with strips of Brussels lace on the bodice of a gown of palest blue. Even Aunt Augusta complimented her on her work.

Later, as they changed for dinner, Isabel exhibited almost as much excitement as Caroline. "I overheard the whole thing. A wonderful result, but Aunt Augusta made ludicrous demands. She made your mother promise to pay for the stable boy and the ponies' food."

The next morning, Caroline truly suffered from a lack of rest. Even after she had gone to bed, no matter how much she longed for sleep, her mind refused to release Thomas Ogden from her consciousness. No matter how much she tried to concentrate on finding a satisfactory solution to her future, she found herself recalling the mischievous twinkle in his eyes, his quick grin, his pointed teasing.

She knew her experience with young men to be extremely limited. Was her reaction to Thomas, so disconcerting in its effects, simply a result of her unfamiliarity with polished gentlemen? Or was the reaction to him and him alone?

She really did not know which was worse. If she reacted with such fluttery giddiness to every fellow who led her out, she would be an utter ninny on the dance floor.

On the other hand, if her feelings applied exclusively to Thomas Ogden, what absurdities did that portend? Aunt Augusta had told her that he had absolutely no prospects at all and that his pretensions to gentlemanly pursuits were dependent upon his gambling take, a less than reliable source of income. Even Caroline knew enough to stay away from gamblers.

After her workout with the ponies, she changed into her morning dress and headed to the pianoforte. Caroline assumed Thomas had joined in the daily quest for trout. With little patience for the boredom of the exercises, she began to grapple with the scales.

"Excuse me, Miss Parker. I assure you I am not trying to intrude upon you without warning."

She jumped at the sound of Thomas's voice from the corner of the room. "I am the one to request your pardon, Captain Ogden. I did not notice you there."

He walked over to the instrument and gave her a rakish grin. "You will not have to endure many performances in public if you offer to play that ditty, Miss Parker."

"The scales? Then I shall do exactly that, Captain Ogden, perform the scales. Tell me, does the *ton* truly enjoy listening to the pitiful performances of young ladies? Please say it is all a delusion."

"I rarely attended musical evenings, but I can tell you they are real enough, though avoided by many young men, if possible."

"Now that Mama and Aunt Augusta have agreed I may take the ponies, I promised to behave myself and try to make a good showing for the Season. But I declare it all seems so stilted."

"Miss Parker, you amaze me. Young ladies usually seem to enjoy every aspect of Society. After all, the entire Season is arranged with the motive of showing them off to their future bridegrooms."

She stood and moved away from the pianoforte. Outside, the March garden looked bleak under a dark, cloudy sky. "That is exactly why I find the Season so daunting. My mother and Aunt Augusta are dedicated to finding me a husband this year." Caroline found the admission amazingly easy to make.

"This year?" He moved to her side, watching her as she gazed out the windows.

"Yes. They expect me to marry by this autumn. In fact, they insist upon it." Desperation edged her voice.

"Families assume daughters will do the usual thing."

"But I do not want to marry."

"What are your alternatives?"

"I have not thought of any yet. But I shall. No one can force me to marry against my will."

"True enough. But what if you want to get married? After all, you might fall in love."

She turned and met his gaze. "I doubt it very much. Anyway, my mother says that love comes after marriage, not before, no matter what the novels say."

"I own I have often heard the same opinion. Highly overrated, love is."

She frowned at him. "Do not tease me, Captain Ogden. What do you know of love anyway? Have you ever been in love?"

"No. Have you?"

She shook her head and spoke softly. "Actually, I rather think I would like to be in love. If the feelings were returned in kind, of course."

"In my own case, I doubt I will ever have the experience."

Something in his tone provoked Caroline. "How would you know? I suppose you London fellows" — what she wanted to say was "fribbles" or "rakehells" or something disparaging — "feign your sensibilities so much that you would hardly know what real feelings are."

Thomas struggled to hide a smile. "I cannot speak for every man in town, but I suspect you are correct in most cases. As for myself, I plead unfamiliarity with any definition of love that relates to my own experience, or shall we say the lack of it?"

Caroline could not help laughing. The thought of such a handsome, genial, and polished young gentleman as Thomas Ogden having no experience with love was indeed far-fetched, if Ned and Simon were even a tiny bit accurate in their tales.

He caught the tenor of her laugh, more than a bit ironic, and he laughed with her. "You will be pleased to know that I do revere my mother, and my brothers rate high in my regard. I am certain that you will have a most successful Season, and if you decide to choose a husband this year, no doubt there will be many excellent prospects for you. Now I shall leave you to perfect those scales and prepare them for a most unusual performance." With a brief bow, he left the room, closing the door behind him.

Caroline stared at the door. If his conversation was any indication, Captain Thomas Ogden was more accomplished at dalliance than anyone she had ever encountered.

When the ladies withdrew from the dining room that evening, Aunt Augusta sent Caroline and Isabel to the music room with Lady Clarissa. "The young men," Augusta intoned, "will not be with us tonight. I have a few things to see to, so I want you to practice your steps with each other. Clarissa will play, and I will look in on you later."

Caroline felt a stab of disappointment.

She had planned to ask Captain Ogden to join them in the dancing. After all, with the steady improvement in his leg, he admitted he needed to polish his steps. She was anxious to continue their morning's conversation. What, she wondered, did young men in London look for in a lady? Could she be esteemed in London without deciding on marriage? In fact, that was exactly what she wanted to do. Her mother and Aunt Augusta would be proud of her, and perhaps they would drop their idea of immediate marriage.

But when she had sneaked off to find him this afternoon, Thomas had been deep in conversation with Uncle Jeremy. Sitting in the bailiff's office, they were talking about sheep, of all things. Caroline had waited for a long time outside, but eventually gave up.

Clarissa smiled at the girls. "Caroline, what are you dreaming about? I think your aunt is flattering you, if a bit indirectly."

"I am sure that Ned, Simon, and Captain Ogden are off to the inn for a little gaming," Caroline speculated.

"And they will have more fun," Isabel added.

But without the fastidious and critical

eye of Aunt Augusta, Caroline and Isabel found the dances quite entertaining, laughing as they mimed the gentleman's role with courteous bowing and affected mannerisms. They were surprised to find themselves comfortable with the steps and enjoying every minute of the music. By the time Aunt Augusta joined them, both young ladies had gained confidence and proficiency.

"I think the girls are about ready for the ballroom, Augusta," Clarissa said.

"Excellent. You know," Augusta repeated for the hundredth time, "you must learn the steps carefully so you have confidence and can hold your head high and smile. Every aspect of your countenance will be noticed. Whatever your mother says, Caroline, you need considerably more practice."

Somehow, Caroline thought, Aunt Augusta managed to squeeze the joy out of everything.

Caroline lingered in the music room, sorting and resorting the music until she heard the others going upstairs to retire. As she had hoped, no one noted her absence. She snuffed the candles, leaving the room lit only by the coals in the fireplace.

Arranging her skirts around her, she sat on the hearth rug. Only a few weeks ago, she had been carefree, satisfied with the accomplishments she now regarded as pitifully meager. Never would she have thought of rebelling against her mother's wishes. Never would she have thought of her future as circumscribed by social conventions she cared nothing for. And never would she have thought her awareness of a certain young man would become so persistent and so irksome.

Staring into the soft glow of the dying fire, she felt troubled. She had been so hen-witted she had hardly given a thought to her future. Only the vaguest notions of her prospects had ever occupied her mind, and now, in the space of a few weeks, the rest of her life would be molded. She would be cast into the hands of a stranger, expected to give him her trust, her affection, and her body. She shuddered at the thought. Though Caroline could not quite visualize the procedure, she knew the meaning of marital rights.

In Isabel's opinion, Caroline would have a splendid time choosing a husband from the many men she would meet at magnificent romantic balls, balls at which swarms of handsome swains would compete for her attention. But why would London gatherings be so different from the local assemblies, where the young men had to be coaxed into dancing by their mamas, while the young ladies on the sidelines carried on animated conversations to show they really did not mind being left out of the festivities?

As for the music and recitations Aunt Augusta insisted she perform, Caroline wagered the average age of gentlemen in attendance would be in the grandfather category.

Caroline twisted a ribbon around her fingers. Perhaps she most feared failure. Novels were full of young ladies who did not take and had to be sent off as governesses or companions. Perhaps such a position was even an option for her, though she had no idea how one found a post, and the thought of spending her life as a quasi-servant had little appeal.

Some of those gloomy stories took place in dark and mysterious castles, full of tormented and sinister characters who threatened the heroines with torturous penalties if they did not succumb to their masters' wicked intents. Hauntingly evil libertines with glittering black eyes pursued innocent young ladies through tortured labyrinths of cold stone. Caroline shuddered, remembering the twisted and satanic satyr in one story, threatening a terrified girl with loathsome and despicable acts, an outrageous fate no one ever detailed.

Caroline recoiled in sudden fear as she heard the door creaking open, slowly and with a definitely ominous rasp. For an instant, as she detected nothing but silence, she held her breath.

"Miss Parker?" Thomas Ogden whispered.

Her heart pounding, her throat tightening, she swallowed hard. "I am here by the fire."

He sat down beside her. "I hope I did not frighten you."

"Well, a little. I was just dreaming."

"About glittering ballrooms and handsome gentlemen?"

She giggled in spite of herself. "Not really. Quite the opposite, in fact."

"Now that sounds rather contrary to your interests."

She changed the subject. "I thought you had gone to the village. In fact, the rumor had you gaming a bit."

"I thought I'd give Simon and Ned a night without me around. Give them the opportunity to see just how well these country fellows can do at cards. I think the two young jackanapes are a bit overconfident of their own abilities. Simon and Ned may have a surprise or two in store."

"You are just as severe as Aunt Augusta in your own way."

"Horrors! That is censure enough to ruin all a fellow's good intentions."

She did not reply, abruptly shy at his nearness. Their arms were only inches apart as they sat side by side facing the glowing remnants of the fire.

"I was waiting for you on the landing when Isabel and the ladies came up. I wanted to tell you how beautifully you dance. I doubt your aunt is very generous with her praise, so . . ."

"What has Ned told you about my dancing?" Caroline suspected Thomas meant to tease her again.

"I would not depend upon Ned or Simon for my opinion on much of anything, Miss Parker. I observed your steps myself this evening."

"You did? How? When?" she breathed, incredulous.

"Let me put it this way. I find my strolls on the terrace quite illuminating here at Sunnyslope."

"You were peeking through the windows!

For shame, Captain Ogden!"

He chuckled. "Merely getting a breath of fresh air. Like the other night, I heard a most engaging voice, this time combined with music. So I was compelled to investigate."

"I see." But she did not see. Why would he care how she danced?

"If I am any judge, you dance splendidly, Miss Parker. Most graceful and charming."

If only he would move away, far enough that she could not feel his soft breath on her cheek.

Instead, he covered her hand with his, causing little tingles to run up and down her spine and her breath to shorten into little sighs. "Our social customs are all wrong, you see. For most men, watching young ladies like you and Isabel dancing together would be much more rewarding than participating themselves."

"Captain Ogden, you embarrass me."

"Miss Parker, that is not my intent. I am merely trying to overpower the effects of your aunt's criticisms. I am certain you will be a success in London."

"I am more convinced I will be an utter antidote." She wanted to move her hand, shift it away from his touch, yet nothing seemed more impossible.

He tightened his grip on her hand and lifted it to his lips. "I consider myself quite thoroughly qualified to judge these matters, indeed far more competent than the esteemed Lady Augusta. That is, if you want a male view."

Caroline felt flattered but even more disconcerted. He kept hold of her hand, and her heart hammered so hard she was sure he could hear its pounding. "I appreciate your good words," she whispered.

Very slowly, he leaned toward her. Ever so slightly, she felt herself swaying nearer. As his lips touched hers, they were so very soft she feared she only imagined his kiss.

His mouth brushed her cheek like feather down and his fingertips caressed the length of her arm. Deep inside, she melted at his touch, and when he kissed her again, she had to stifle the urge to wrap her arms around his shoulders and press her body to his.

His gentle smile made her breath catch in her throat. "Now, I think Oberon and Titania will have their revenge on me if I do not let you get to bed."

As in a daze, Caroline rose and walked with him, her hand tucked under his arm, upstairs to the hall near her room.

Again, he lifted her hand to his lips.

Their gentle, velvety touch made her knees tremble, and she bit her lip to keep from sighing out loud.

"Good night, Miss Parker," he whispered.

"Good night," she murmured.

Thomas leaned against a table in the shadowed hallway for a few moments. My God, what was he thinking of? Flattering a sweet young chit like Caroline was one thing; kissing her was quite another, absolutely asinine and quite beyond the limit. In just weeks, both of them would be embroiled in London's spring rituals, both indulging in the custom honored only by its perpetual repetition: making a rich match.

Shaking his head, Thomas walked to his room and stretched out on the bed fully clothed. Why his old leg wound chose this moment to ache so dreadfully he could not imagine. Unless the pain came from the same ineffectual fretting that made his head swim every time the thought of London drawing rooms came to mind.

If he and Caroline had stayed one more minute before that dying fire, he could not have resisted taking her in his arms. But he dared not give in to his feelings. Too much was at stake for both of them. For now, she had some alternatives, while he had none. Caroline could find a wealthy man and be set for life.

Everything had changed for him, Thomas thought. Without any warning, he faced responsibilities far above his capacity to manage. At Aldonhurst, countless families suffered under the old marquess and his cheating rotter of a bailiff. Could he give those tenants some hope for the future?

Last year at this time he was reckless and bold, a neck or nothing at racing horses or playing cards, arrogantly confident of his skills. Why was he different now?

It was an odd feeling, this underlying emotion of caring. Oh, he had cared for his men in Spain; they had cared for each other, for their lives depended on each other. That was different.

After he returned he had cared for no one, even himself some of the time. Of course he did not wish to disgrace his mother or his brother Lionel. And he certainly felt he had justly earned the esteem of some younger fellows with his skill at cards, his fine clothes, and his facility with the wrong kind of women.

No, nothing in his life had prepared him for the affection, regard, and strong sense of responsibility he felt toward the marquess and the people at Aldonhurst. The depth and strength of his feelings came as a real surprise, and not necessarily a welcome one. He cared for the marquess, he cared for the property and the heritage, he cared for the tenants and for Josh.

But he was helpless to improve anyone's lot in life if he had no money. There it was again: the ignominy of becoming a fortune hunter in the marriage mart.

Perhaps he should return to the gaming tables. But he knew that his run of extraordinary luck would not last forever. As soon as he had to have the money, he lost his edge with the other players, many of whom had very deep pockets.

Thomas rolled off the bed and limped to the window. A half-moon cast its cold light on the serene fields and woods of Sunnyslope. Lord Barstow controlled a prosperous estate of thousands of acres encompassing hundreds of people. Every day Thomas observed the earl conferring with his bailiff, inspecting the operation of each ingredient in the vast stew of his domain. Perhaps, Thomas mused, Lord Barstow would take him on his daily rounds for the next week or two. Watching at close hand might provide a useful lesson.

Six

Lady Clarissa paced her bedroom, suffering one of her frequent bouts of guilt. What had once seemed the proper thing to do for Caroline was now just a matter of having her own selfish way. Yet nothing was more reasonable than having her daughter settled. She could never confide in Augusta, and Letitia barely coped with her own megrims.

She needed to confide in someone and went to the billiard room to seek her brother.

"Clarissa, my dear, how are you?" Lord Barstow asked. "We haven't had much opportunity to talk. I am afraid that when Augusta takes over, I retreat." Lord Barstow and Lady Clarissa were long accustomed to dealing with their imperious elder sister.

Clarissa smiled and patted his arm. "I am fine, Jeremy. Just fine. And I am sorry to be the cause of all this fuss in your house."

"Sunnyslope is your home, too, and Augusta's, for all that I complain."

"Yes, but all this activity has put dear Letitia rather into a decline, I fear."

"Oh, Letitia is strong enough when she chooses to be, you know. But our dear sister thoroughly intimidates her. Always has."

"Augusta's bark is worse than her bite, as they say. And I am sure she'll do well by Caroline. She seems to have excellent connections in the city."

"Please advise me if you do not wish to answer this question, my dear sister, but I do not understand why you are so anxious to promote Caroline's marriage. It seems excessively hurried to expect her to find a husband for life in a single Season, though of course I know many chits do exactly that."

Lady Clarissa turned away and walked to the window. She gazed out into the darkness, seeing only her blurry reflection in the glass. "Can you keep my confidence?"

"Clarissa, I am your brother, your only brother. I would never violate your trust."

"But what I am about to tell you might change how you feel toward me. I know it would change Augusta's views."

"Nothing will change my regard for you."

"I hope not, but regardless of your opinion of what I plan to do, promise me that you will not stand in my way, Jeremy."

"I promise." His sympathetic expression gave her courage.

"Caroline must make a good match and be settled by fall. Because . . ." She hesitated, then took a deep breath. "I intend to accompany a man to the continent. The war is winding down and when the peace conference begins, I shall go with him and live as his wife."

"But . . ."

"Please, Jeremy, hear me out. I love him and he loves me. He is tied to a wife who is very ill and needs constant nursing care, and he cannot divorce her. We are prepared to live with the scandal that will attach to our names. But I cannot ruin my daughter."

She turned to look at Jeremy, but found him slumped in his chair, staring at the floor. Tears ran down her cheeks. "Oh, brother dear, I am being so selfish. I do not expect you to understand, but believe me, without him I simply cannot go on."

Lord Barstow sighed, then held out his arms to his sister. "You are correct. I don't understand, but I cannot condemn you. Though others will find your actions thoroughly reprehensible."

Clarissa dried her eyes. "And you will suffer, too, all of you. The gossips will have a wonderful time. Caroline will certainly be hurt, but at least she will be settled. Once the initial rumormongering subsides, she will be able to go on as before. As long as she is already married. If she is not, she might end up on the shelf forever or take a lesser offer — or even . . ."

Clarissa was grateful for her brother's strong arms of comfort.

Thomas followed Caroline into the stables in the early morning, surprised to see her usually cheery visage looked troubled.

"Good morning, Captain Ogden." She tried in vain to bring a smile to her lips.

He smiled at her with what he hoped was a compassionate expression. "Miss Parker, is something amiss? You look sadly distraught."

"You must excuse me, Captain Ogden. I beg your indulgence. It was quite unmannerly of me yesterday to plague you with my problems. Most unseemly."

"Please do not be upset. As a matter of fact, upon reflection, I assume your point of view on the Season might be customary for many young ladies. I have so little experience with the feminine point of view that I thought every one of you would be eager and delighted to participate in the marriage mart."

"I should not burden you with worries about my prospects."

"Believe me, I understand your point of view, better than you can imagine." Thomas stopped himself before he blurted out his own circumstance.

Caroline did not meet his eyes and continued to crinkle a ribbon dangling from her bonnet. "I have resigned myself to the Season. I will try to be accommodating, but the marriage part is unimaginable. The whole marriage mart process seems very cold and cruel. Emphasizes so many of the wrong qualities."

He spoke with conviction. "I agree. Today's marriages are no better, based as they are on this charade of courtship, than the arranged marriages of our grandparents."

"Now you sound like my mother. She married a much older man, my father, and grew to love him very much. She, too, points out that so many of our current fads in courtship are not conducive to developing the best kind of knowledge about one another."

"True. One cannot stand up with any young lady more than twice in an evening, or one is considered betrothed." Thomas felt a stab of conscience. She had bravely confided in him, and now he wanted to confide in her. He yearned for her approval, but found no honor in his purpose. Would she not think less of him if she knew?

Caroline's frowning mood did not change. "Courting must be much easier for a man."

Suddenly serious, he shook his head. "It is not. Not in the slightest, Miss Parker."

"And this time you truly speak from experience, I suppose?" Her tone was mildly mocking.

"Not yet," he mumbled, hesitating. She had been excruciatingly honest, so why shouldn't he? "In other years, I avoided any consideration of the parson's mousetrap. But this year will be different. You see, my mother has set me to winning a fortune in the marriage mart."

"A fortune?"

He stood beside her, staring into the misty chill. "Precisely. I will become one of those notorious fortune hunters you have heard so much about."

"Then you and I, sir, seem cut from the

same bolt indeed. I am to be sold to the highest bidder, assuming he meets my Aunt Augusta's lofty standards. Perhaps I should be relieved to hear that another has the same predicament."

"My mother tells me that I should look for a young lady with a large inheritance and strength of character, perhaps not a beauty but with impeccable bloodlines. Back again to the model of choosing a horse, I fear."

"Excuse me for asking, Captain Ogden, but why does your mother insist that you marry a lady of wealth?"

He looked into her wide eyes, as blue as a summery sky. "I have told no one this story, and I own I find the facts rather farfetched myself. You see, it seems I am about to inherit property from a distant relative, property currently without much income."

Caroline's surprise showed in her face.

Haltingly at first, then with greater strength, he told her about the old marquess, the ramshackle estate, and even his promise to reestablish the dynasty.

"Which puts me in the same auction ring as you," he finished. "All I will know about a young lady is what my mother chooses to tell me. Assuming, of course, that she is not an object of gossip in the clubs, which hardly seems likely."

"I will be the one worrying about gossip, perhaps started by you."

He grinned ruefully. "Not any more. If you promise to keep secret my fortune-hunting mission, I will protect your exploits as a male curricle driver."

"True." Her smile beamed delighted relief. "We will each have a concern for the other's status. Do you think we will attend the same parties in town?"

"I am sure of it. My mother will not be so strict with Simon, but she has told me I am expected to escort her to as many balls as possible. She is opening my brother's town house and Simon is staying there. I have insisted on keeping my own rooms a few streets away."

"But why —"

The arrival of Becky with an armload of puppies interrupted the conversation. "Aunt Augusta is looking for you, Caroline. She was heading for the music room, where you are supposed to be practicing, she says."

"Oh, dear, I have lost track of the time." Pulling on her cloak, Caroline ran toward the kitchen garden entrance to the house.

★ ★ ★

Caroline gazed at herself in the cheval glass as Peg, daughter of the estate carpenter, brushed her honey curls.

"They say, miss, young ladies in town have cut off their long tresses."

"However did you hear such a thing?" Caroline asked.

Peg drew Caroline's hair high, then piled the coil at the back of her head and arranged a few curls around her face. "I heard that from Lady Augusta's abigail, and Mrs. Beecham's daughter said the same thing after she visited Bath."

"Do you think I should?" Peg had a way with hair, Caroline thought. The arrangement of her curls looked quite becoming.

"You be the one to decide, miss." She wove ribbons in three shades of pink into Caroline's hair, matching the trim on her ivory muslin gown.

"I suppose I should wait until I arrive in London and see how others are wearing their hair," Caroline mused out loud. "I can always have it cut off, but not the other way around."

Peg chuckled. "That's fer sure, Miss Caroline." The maidservant tidied up the dressing table, humming as she left the room. Caroline thought she recognized the sonatina she had been practicing that afternoon on the pianoforte.

Peg definitely angled to go along to London, Caroline thought. The young woman was not trained as a ladies' maid, but she would be welcome, an agreeable source of common sense.

Caroline sighed and stared into the glass. The newly embellished gown flattered her. The glow of the ribbon rosettes around the neckline complimented her rosy complexion. Only to herself would she admit how pleased she was that Ellis's secret potion really minimized the freckles on her nose.

How would she compare to the other young ladies being presented in London? Perhaps she should come right out and ask Thomas Ogden. After their talk this morning, she felt like she had forged a sort of bond with him.

She would surely meet a few young ladies, and one of them might be just right for Thomas. That task might occasionally divert her attention from worrying about which gentlemen were worth knowing. The next opportunity she had to talk with Captain Ogden, she would suggest such a scheme.

After dinner, Lady Augusta excused

Caroline and Isabel from their dancing, sending them off to practice their French lessons.

"The way Aunt Augusta hates Napoléon, I am surprised she insists we learn his language," Caroline commented.

"*Exactement, m'amie,*" replied Isabel, who tended to sprinkle French expressions into her everyday speech.

"Why are the numbers so difficult?" Caroline complained. "*Un* to *vingt-et-un* are easy enough, but seventy, eighty, and ninety are absurd."

After practicing the days of the week and months of the year, Isabel declared herself finished for the evening. "I think we should join the young men in the billiard room."

"You go ahead. I shall run through my music lesson once more." Isabel shrugged and hurried off. Caroline hoped Thomas would have had enough billiards for the evening; he might come to the music room if he heard her playing, and she was anxious to resume their conversation.

Within the half hour, her wish was fulfilled. She answered a soft scratching on the door with a sincere, "Come in, please."

Captain Ogden stood behind her as she finished the piece, then applauded lightly. "Your diligence is most commendable,

Miss Parker. Apparently your aunt's discipline is paying off. That sounded quite respectable."

"Feeble praise, I daresay."

"Pardon me, I did not intend an offense, truly I did not."

She left the bench and sat near the fire. "Oh, I am not offended in the least. I am quite realistic in assessing my advancement, and believe it or not, I have improved vastly. Soon I will play that song and the sonatina without any errors. You see, I refuse to disgrace myself or my mother."

"Excellent. That spirit becomes you."

"Captain Ogden, I have had an idea about your search for a suitable match."

"Suitable is a fine term, indicating fortune, wealth, and riches, if I may be redundant."

"Perhaps when I meet a suitable young lady, I could tell you about her. You would not want a wife who is self-centered or vain or shallow. If you give me the name of a young lady who interests you, I could judge her suitability."

"Yes. Capital idea, Miss Parker."

"Aunt Augusta says many girls have money these days, so you might as well choose from among the rich ones who have other pleasing qualities."

He grinned and made a little bow. "And I could tell you just how arrogant or ineffectual your suitors really are."

"Oh dear, I cannot imagine having actual suitors."

"Miss Parker, I assure you there will be many interested in you. And I will endeavor to identify those gentlemen whose habits are most congenial, as well as warning you against those who have bad habits such as gambling or drinking to excess."

"Take care that checking out the unsavory spots does not take up all your time. You will have to save some time for wooing."

"Yes, I suppose so."

"Though I perceive you already have extensive practice, however often you demur of knowing anything about romance." Surprised at her own boldness, she felt a blush warm her cheeks.

Thomas looked at her with a little nod, unable to prevent a grin stealing onto his lips. "Miss Parker, I find my vocabulary to be lacking. There must be a feminine rendering of the term 'rascal' or 'rogue.' Surely 'scoundrel' would not suffice for a young lady, and 'minx' is far too amiable for such a saucy lass as you."

"On the contrary, Captain Ogden. I am merely surmising that one who is held in such high regard by my cousin Ned could not be other than a skilled man about town."

"I am quite sure the young men greatly exaggcrate my reputation. Nevertheless, I find your plan of mutual observation most intriguing. We shall make quite as companionable a pair as the estimable Oberon and Titania."

"Then we are agreed?" she asked.

"Quite so." He poured two glasses of sherry. "Now just a brief toast to seal our contract."

Caroline's thoughts seesawed back and forth. At dawn, she was exhausted but unable to sleep. Slowly she dressed and went to the stables, silently confiding in her ponies, creatures that could give her no answers but immense solace. She wondered if Captain Ogden would join her on the morning drive, but he did not appear, and her attention to the ponies drove him temporarily out of her thoughts for a few hours.

At the table that evening, Caroline found herself watching Thomas Ogden, practically staring at him, in fact. Luckily Aunt Augusta was holding forth about the importance of some people known as the lady patronesses of a place called Almack's. The gist certainly made no sense to Caroline, but the subject seemed important to the others.

The captain was the kind of man she would like to know better, she thought as he smiled at some remark Ned made. Thomas had a lively mind, willing to take on even Augusta. He had no fortune, and the rumors of his gambling . . . well, they were much more than rumors. Simon and Ned left no doubt that he was skilled at cards. Was he typical of the young men she would meet in town, a dandy at heart, simply trifling with life?

Caroline welcomed Captain Ogden's company the next morning. Their conversation as they drove revealed a more serious side to him when she persuaded him to speak of his army experience, a topic he obviously approached with reluctance.

"Really, I am not a shrinking violet afraid to hear about violence. Please tell me."

He looked far off into the distance and took a deep sigh. "I bought my colours when I was barely out of Eton, much too young to understand what war was all about. Napoléon-hating was hardly an uncommon attribute among my friends. Before I knew what I was doing, I shipped off to Portugal."

She urged him to continue. "And?"

"We spent months milling about, trying to conduct training . . ." His voice trailed off and he gazed away again.

"Please go on, Captain Ogden," she implored.

After a long pause, he sighed deeply. "War is a thoroughly foul occupation, short spurts of absolute bloody terror divided by long, tedious stretches of utter boredom."

His jaw was tense with strain and his hands were clenched into white-knuckled fists. "In the first engagements, not much more than skirmishes, I had not a scratch. But at Talavera, a shell exploded in the first hour, and next thing I knew I was being dragged to a pile of dead and wounded. I never knew exactly what happened, but I probably owe my life to some poor bastard stacking up the dead. I must have moaned, and he searched until he found me half alive. I never knew who he was." He sighed again, and wiped perspiration from his brow despite the chill air.

"Excuse me, Miss Parker. I apologize for saying far too much."

"Oh, no, Captain Ogden. I want to hear more. How long before you recovered?"

He began quietly, but again his voice grew tortured. "The doctors sent me back to England to mend, but the army would not let me go back to the fight. I received a post in the war office, sitting at a desk. I could not stand the ignorance there. No one knew what was happening on the peninsula. The way they treated Lord Wellesley's requests made me sick. The politicians blame the generals for every setback, but they and Prinny are happy enough to take the credit for victories. As a mere captain, I was much too junior to have any influence, so eventually I gave it up." Thomas's expression was dismal, his voice barely audible.

"You must have been incredibly frustrated."

"Yes. I am not proud that I abandoned the effort to change their attitudes, but I found it hopeless."

She set about cheering him then, diverting his attention to the ponies. By the time they returned to the stables, he had been again in good spirits.

Thomas Ogden had seen the worst of

life, men killing one another in savage violence. She, on the other hand, had known
the glittering world of diplomacy and the
rustic existence of the English countryside.
She understood his cynicism. For him,
finding a purposeful, fulfilling life might be
difficult.

Seven

Thomas sat on a bench in the stable polishing the already bright buckles on the ponies' harness. Less than a week remained before they all were to leave for London.

Caroline braided Oberon's mane. "Captain, what does it mean to be a marquess?"

His brief laugh rang with cynical overtones. "Damned if I know, begging your pardon, Miss Parker, other than inheriting worthless property and being called Lord Aldonhurst. Among the consequences will be a higher rank than my elder brother. My mother says she hopes Lionel does not find out until the old marquess dies. Keeps peace in the family, don't you know? Rather too bad, since I have grown quite fond of being a rackety younger brother."

"How can your brother be a viscount and you become a marquess?"

"We have different fathers. The fifth Viscount Pemstead was mother's first husband; Lionel is the sixth viscount. Simon and I are the result of her second marriage. My father died when I was fifteen, and he told me almost nothing about the Marquess of Aldonhurst. Father never contemplated being a part of the succession."

Caroline tightened thread around the last braid. "Will you become excessively top lofty? Perhaps Aunt Augusta should teach you the proper haughty way with a quizzing glass so you can stare down any undeserving chit."

"Good lord, Miss Parker, do not tell your Aunt Augusta, or I will be done for! As things stand now, I am nobody, and I do not think she approves of me." He knew she did not.

"She certainly will not if she suspects your pockets are to let."

Knowing Lady Augusta, he could already guarantee she knew his worth to the ha'penny. "I hate the thought of marrying for money. Of course, I can hardly be a proper marquess without some funds. Lord Aldonhurst's estate lies in shambles."

"Will you be able to straighten things out and bring it back to prosperity?" She patted the pony's sleek neck.

"I plan to do just that. But I need money to make improvements, perhaps even innovations. I talked with your uncle, Lord Barstow. He recommended some articles on new agricultural advances. Unfortunately such improvements could take many years. I need funds to get started. Hence, the heiress."

Caroline gazed at him thoughtfully. "Our dilemmas are really quite different, are they not? You will manage a lady's fortune, and I will be managed by my husband."

He frowned and stared down at the straw-covered floor. "Marriage for a man is entirely different than for a lady; a lady is looking for love and kindness. A man is looking for different qualities: the ability to supervise a household and mother a family."

"Companionship?"

"I suppose . . . of course, companionship."

She removed her gloves and inspected her neat hands. "I know why you think women look for love."

"Why?"

"Because otherwise, without love, why would a woman accept such an uneven bargain? There has to be a hope, something beyond mere dynastic procreation."

"Ah, Miss Parker, then you are admitting that love is a fantasy?"

"Of course not. I am saying that your point of view is entirely different than mine. But even you cannot deny that love would be a particularly appealing ingredient of marriage."

"I'd say nothing of the kind. Love is imaginary, more make-believe than real."

Caroline closed the stall door. "Mama says love often comes after marriage and grows through the years."

"That assumes that you like the person more and more as you get to know him better. What if you take him in dislike? Instead of love growing, then, a mild aversion could grow into loathing. I've seen that happen, all right."

"I suppose it happens, probably often." She picked up a bridle from a hook above him. "If you do not believe in love, Captain Ogden, then what do you believe?"

Thomas paused. He wished the circumstances were such that he could simply confess his real feelings, his feelings of fondness for her. But he did not meet her family's requirements. He dared not let his affection for Caroline develop into love. He had no choice but to fall back on his cavalier denials. "I will marry someone I respect, who will make a good mother."

"But if you do not love her, how could you . . ." Her voice trailed off.

"This is hardly a subject your aunt

148

would approve of, my dear. But be assured I will do my duty by my wife."

"Without love, it seems an empty, joyless act."

He felt a chill in the pit of his stomach. How could he extricate himself from this conversation? "Miss Parker, many men seek their joy in places other than the marriage bed."

Her voice was indignant. "I am not so green as to doubt that, but I should not like to find it true of my husband."

He shrugged and examined another section of the harness. When he looked up, she stared into the distance, a wistful look on her lovely face. She held him in some affection, too, that he knew. But just as he could not pursue her, so she could not consider him as a potential match. Perhaps it was time to squelch her nascent feelings for him before they grew any stronger.

He stood and hung the harness on its peg. "You may think me an unsavory libertine, but I cannot see why marriage completely has to tie a fellow's hands. Or any other part of his anatomy."

Her mouth dropped wide open. "Thomas Ogden! You are a heartless rake!"

He took no pleasure in her shock at his

crudeness. Or his lies. But he was surprised at her sudden burst of laughter.

"Captain, I predict you will receive your just deserts someday. Jealousy can lead to very rash behavior."

He shrugged again. "Miss Parker, I think you have listened to gossip you should not have heard."

"And I have also heard other stories, about how much Lady Sachet might wish her husband to find a new mistress. She is tired of him, you see, and has interests of her own. Perhaps you will be the victim of such a scheme. Or . . ."

He held up his hand. "Do not say another word! This is most improper, and I will have to report you to Lady Augusta if it continues."

He had to admit Miss Parker gave as good as she got.

The next morning, a late March rain drenched the Sunnyslope park. Isabel and Caroline sat in the morning room and glowered at their samplers. Caroline set her piece on the table, walked to the window, and gazed at the gloomy garden.

She could not rid herself of the distress she felt after her conversation with Thomas on marital faithfulness. Why, she asked herself, did his attitude matter to her? She would not be his wife, however pleasing she usually found his company. His candor should not have surprised her, after the nature of their bargain to assist each other in finding wealthy matches.

She gave a long sigh of frustration.

Isabel looked up from her work. "What is wrong, Caro?"

Caroline sat again and picked up her sampler. "When we get to London, I hope you will not be disappointed when I go out in the evening and you have to stay home."

"I will not mind. Aunt Augusta says I will be ever so ready next year."

"Is that all Aunt Augusta says?"

"Of course she is going to continue our dancing lessons and this dratted stitching and the pianoforte and everything. I want to see the sights of London ever so much. Just think of it. We will buy hats and ribbons and lacy mitts. We will go to Gunter's for ices, and perhaps to the theater."

"Aunt Augusta considers the theater to be a bad influence on morality, you know."

"Oh, anyway, it will be very exciting. I can help you dress for the balls, and you will tell me everything, absolutely everything about the handsome men and beautiful gowns."

As they heard steps approaching the morning room, they both grabbed up their needlework.

Lady Clarissa smiled as she came into the morning room. "I am delighted to see you girls being so diligent. Later, Caroline, I hope you will help Peg pack your trunks. She has little experience in being an abigail, but she will have to do."

Caroline nodded. "Peg will do fine. She has the makings of a passable lady's maid."

"Augusta received at least four letters this morning, and I believe the news, whatever it was, made her happy."

"Or perhaps she nipped at the sherry?" Caroline could not resist the temptation.

Her mother was truly dismayed. "Caroline! Such disrespect. I do not expect to hear such talk again." But a hint of a smile and a distinct gleam in her eye gave Lady Clarissa away.

Isabel's failure to suppress her giggles sent all three into peals of laughter.

Clarissa hugged her daughter. "You will have a wonderful time in London. Besides Aunt Augusta and Uncle Barnaby and me, you will have Isabel and Ned and Peg, and the ponies, too."

"I know, Mama. I try not to be fainthearted, but there's something so crass about offering oneself so obviously."

"Would you rather have no say, an arranged marriage? Augusta is right. You have the breeding and the polish to take your place in Society. With the right husband . . ."

"Please, no quibbling, Mama. I am going to try. I promised."

"I know, dear." Clarissa smiled at Caroline. "And I am sure you will make an excellent choice."

The next day, Lady Augusta led the ladies from the luncheon table with an air of particular gravity. When they were settled in the drawing room, she produced a sheet of heavy cream vellum. "I am assured that any of these three eligible gentlemen would be appropriate and probably would make an early offer. I have carefully culled the recommendations of my most intimate friends, ladies whose connections are from only the highest circles."

She opened the sheet and read off a name. "Sir Reginald Sedgewick. A recently widowed baronet with an enormous fortune. Though his wealth came from the China trade in the last century, the Sedgewicks have been landed and gentrified for several generations. Sir Reginald is about thirty-five, had no children with his late wife, and is definitely on the search for a young wife with whom he wishes to fill his nursery."

Caroline wanted to sink into the cushions and disappear from sight. Breeding stock, she thought.

"Charles, Lord Graham," Aunt Augusta continued, "the eldest son and heir to Baron Poynton, is about to turn thirty, and is said to be under parental orders to set up a nursery. Charles's mother, Lady Poynton, will be a force to reckon with. She will probably make the choice of the bride, and she will look over this year's crop of eligible females carefully."

She would not have to worry about Lord Graham then, Caroline thought. There were bound to be other girls far more eligible and willing for the countess to scrutinize. But the idea of acquiring a mother-in-law to go along with a husband added to her recalcitrant temper.

Aunt Augusta gave no import to Caroline's lack of response. "Gilbert Cunningham, the Earl of Longbury, is the third and most preferred candidate. I have known him all his life, since his mother, the countess, is a bosom bow of mine. I find him a dear boy, despite his unfortunate stutter."

And his tendency to paunchiness, his receding chin, his already thinning brown hair, and his apparent lack of consequence, Caroline thought. She had met the unimposing Gilbert a year ago at an assembly, and she knew him to be a poor dancer, clumsy horseman, and awkward driver. But she said nothing.

"I believe dear Gilbert is bound to be an easy conquest, if you apply yourself, Caroline. All three prospects have at least five thousand per year. I am told there are several men in town seeking an alliance who are not so plump in the pocket. These gentlemen must be avoided at all cost, as are those whose backgrounds are not thoroughly familiar to me. There will be no occasion to take up with a racier crowd."

Caroline did not know whether to laugh or weep. What an array of choices. Of course Lady Augusta would not consider Thomas Ogden. He had no title that her aunt knew of, and no future prospects. Aunt Augusta questioned even his faultless social manners, since Ned and Simon considered him a prime role model: a notorious rake, gambler, and man about town.

Once Caroline had overheard Aunt

Augusta excoriating Thomas to Lady Clarissa. "I do not doubt that his name is often linked with members of the muslin set. Older men might be forgiven their little flings, but for one so young, it is outrageous. He is entirely the wrong kind of young man to have around Caroline."

Caroline had been surprised to hear her mother's defense. "I disagree, Augusta. I find him very polite and a true gentleman. I am hopeful that he will be on hand to dance with Caroline at some routs. And there is another important consideration."

"What is that, sister dear?"

"If Captain Ogden is known to be without prospects, and he is often seen with Caroline, others will not be inclined to fancy her a fortune hunter. But at least we agree Captain Ogden is not to be encouraged."

Recalling that exchange made Caroline frown. She looked up to see her mother, Isabel, and Aunt Augusta staring at her. "Excuse me, I am afraid I was dreaming."

Clarissa spoke gently. "Augusta asked what you thought of her suggestions."

"Oh, yes. Thank you so much for your assiduous efforts, Aunt." Obviously from Lady Augusta's sour expression, Caroline's attempt at enthusiasm had fallen far short of expectations.

***

Caroline and Captain Ogden met in the stables the morning of the day he and Simon were to leave for London.

Her spirits had not improved. "Yesterday, Aunt Augusta presented her list of Eligibles."

"Eligibles?" Thomas asked. "She already chose for you?"

Caroline tried to keep the disgust out of her tone. "Precisely. She found three gentlemen with all the proper characteristics; that is, money, social standing, money, family connections, and money. All of them sound gruesome when Aunt Augusta describes them."

"My mother also has suggestions about suitable connections for me with exactly the same qualities."

"So I have the Eligibles, and you will have the Suitables on your mother's list."

"Tell me who the Eligibles are. I may already know them."

Caroline gave Thomas the three names, and indeed, he knew two of them. "Sir Reginald is not among my acquaintances, but I will make some inquiries. Now as to my very succinct list, I wish I could remember the names my mother mentioned.

Perhaps you will meet various young ladies who might do, heiresses or those with a vast dowry. Are we not a fine pair, looking for money and expecting to find congenial *partis* as well? How presumptuous."

"I keep hoping that if we help each other, Captain Ogden, the result will be endurable."

"You have my word that I will learn all I can about the Eligibles and look for any additional candidates as well."

Caroline hesitated, then plunged ahead. "Captain, I feel I must warn you that for ladies like my mother and Aunt Augusta, any hint of gambling or other questionable behavior would spoil a gentleman's chances. I hope you will not, ah . . ."

His grin stopped her. "Miss Parker, I have made much the same pledge to my mother. At least for the next few months, I will be a pattern card of respectability."

"I am glad to hear it. When do you leave for town?"

"In two or three days, only a few ahead of your departure. Are you packed?"

She shrugged. "I am in no hurry. But Isabel is terribly excited. She is sure I will meet a rich and handsome gentleman who will fall in love with me."

"Have I not convinced you that love is

out of the question, superfluous, only a pipe dream?"

"You will never convince me, so you might as well stop trying. I believe in love, though I do not think love is something I can seek now."

His only reply was a crooked smile.

"I have not actually decided to marry. I am sure there are alternatives if I can only think of them. Too bad you will not be a rich marquess with a huge estate. Then I could come and raise my ponies on your property and pay you rent."

"Miss Parker, I can think of no better solution for your problems than to come and live with me."

She could not prevent an exclamation of shock. "That was not what I had in mind, Captain Ogden!" Her cheeks colored with a becoming pink.

"Every young lady approaching her first Season should have at least one offer before she arrives in London."

She could not help laughing. "That is not what Aunt Augusta meant by an offer! Of that I am perfectly confident."

Eight

In the bedroom they shared in London, Isabel fluffed out the sarsanet overskirt of Caroline's ball gown and held up a pair of long ivory kid gloves. "A perfect match, cousin dear."

"Indeed they should be. I carried along a swatch of the silk from the bodice."

"You clever thing. I will remember that when my turn comes."

Caroline laughed. "Just remember that you must wear white. If I had listened to your advice, I would be presented to the Queen in crimson or peacock blue, and Aunt Augusta would tumble into severe apoplexy."

"Would that be a bad thing? Poor Mama would not miss her, that's certain."

"For shame, you imp." Caroline carefully replaced a feathered bonnet in its box and opened a fan of creamy silk, its ivory sticks encrusted with tiny pearls. She peeped over the edge and fluttered her eyelashes at Isabel. "Tell me, my dear Lord Fuss-bottom, how long do you think my esteemed cousin Lady Isabel will reside in Newgate Prison for causing the demise of her aunt?"

"Just the thought of prison makes me hungry. There must be some sweets in the kitchen. Something Ellis will not know about and tattle to Aunt Augusta. Back in a few minutes." Isabel closed the door behind her without a sound. Most of the servants at Barstow House in Berkeley Square were afraid of both Lady Augusta and her wily maid, Ellis, who related their every activity to her mistress. Little escaped Ellis's beady glare, and nothing was overlooked by Lady Augusta. An undusted sconce or a spot of soil on a hem, a crooked fork in a place setting or a fingerprint on a silver server, all were deemed worthy of a reprimand.

But even in the company of her formidable aunt, Caroline caught some of Isabel's enthusiasm for London. Caroline adored their blue-and-white bedroom, indeed every room of the town house. The city was noisy, crowded, dirty — and thoroughly thrilling. People, vehicles, and animals of constantly changing varieties crowded the streets. Each excursion grew more fascinating than the last. The shopping trips almost made up for the tedium of fitting after fitting at the modiste.

Although Lady Augusta made her disapproval of the pony-training scheme quite well known, Lady Clarissa prevailed, and the ponies were comfortably bedded in the mews. Their first outings in the London streets had gone well, though Caroline felt the ponies might be as overwhelmed by the clamor and throngs as she was.

Today, after their shopping expedition, both Aunt Augusta and Lady Clarissa had retired to their rooms for a rest, declaring themselves utterly exhausted. Alone, the two young ladies opened and admired the boxes of treasure deposited on Caroline's bed by the footman.

Caroline donned the chip straw bonnet and turned before the cheval glass, admiring the broad pink ribbons and silk flowers decorating the brim. The flattering hat's pale pink roses looked so real she expected them to have a fragrance. As the weather warmed toward summer, she could wear the bonnet while driving in the park. The ponies would be at their highstepping best, and she even visualized a strolling gentleman raising his hat in salute.

Next she fingered the peacock feathers decorating a hat designed to match her green carriage dress, a truly elegant confection her mother longed to share. She admired the graceful sweep of the feathers, then frowned at her mirror image. They had been in London barely two weeks, and already she had disregarded her mission to find an appropriate alternative to marriage.

How easily she was amused, Caroline thought, how easily she slipped into the excitement of town sights and out of concern for her own future. Yet even her most intense powers of observation today would have yielded her little. The modistes and seamstresses had abilities far beyond her own, and that life hardly appealed to her. Imagine endeavoring to satisfy imperious, haughty, and overbearing ladies like her aunt! She might as well be resigned to becoming a companion to some rich old dragon. At least then the complaints would come from only one source.

Honestly, was not marriage the best option? What other life could offer her any security? Yet, marriage without love . . . indeed, a conundrum. Caroline did not want to marry unless she was in love.

The only man who attracted her was Thomas Ogden, who was in precisely the same situation she was. Thomas made clear his wife might as well know from the start he would pursue other interests. Anyway, he needed a wife to finance his estate, run his household, and fill his nursery, while he sought his pleasures elsewhere. With his fine title and his property restored to prosperity with his wife's fortune, he could flit around the country to shoot and hunt, sail and fish, with any companions he desired, male or female.

The thought disgusted her. His wife would sit home and supervise the children and probably superintend the servants, tenants, and even the livestock.

If she married a man like Thomas, she would not share him. Not for an instant! She was much too jealous.

Isabel came back into their room with a large hatbox in her arms.

Caroline forced herself to push thoughts of Thomas Ogden out of her mind. "Did you bring the entire kitchen?" she asked with forced cheeriness. "Or simply a whole roasted piglet?"

Isabel lifted out a plump little pie. "It was the only box large enough for these strawberry tarts. They are perfectly scrumptious."

Caroline took a tart and savored its juicy sweetness. "Delicious," she confirmed. "We'll miss these at tea, but if we should have callers, I would probably dump one in my lap — or perhaps in Aunt's. How fetching she would look with red juice all over her bosom."

The two smiled at the vision, but were too busy enjoying their tarts to embellish further.

After a second helping, Isabel pushed the box aside. "I may have another later. Now, Caro, have you met all of the Eligibles yet?"

"By the end of this week. Aunt Augusta planned her campaign like a Wellington. She told me that the only gentlemen I should consider must have the highest possible characters. And I should never be seen at any soiree unsuitable to the highest sticklers of the *haut ton*. There will be no theater and no opera."

Caroline imitated her aunt's haughty demeanor. " 'Quite unsuitable for young ladies. This is a serious business, Miss, and we are operating with several disadvantages. Besides having neither money nor accomplishments, you have hoydenish habits. You must set a good example for Lady Isabel and learn to use proper discipline with your abigail. Peg is much too countrified to attend you, but since she has such a way with hair, we will save considerable expense.' "

"With *saving* the important goal here," Isabel added, laughing. "I heard her say I came along because 'the chit needs quite a bit of polish.' Can you imagine?"

"Only too well. She says exactly the same of me."

Caroline knew her aunt planned to devote their first few weeks in town to a round of calls and afternoons spent receiving, renewing old acquaintances and lining up names for ball invitations. Lady Augusta made arrangements for Caroline's presentation at Court, chose the date of her ball, and secured vouchers for Almack's. Caroline never doubted that by the time the Season got into full swing, no one who mattered in London could ignore either Lady Augusta Stolper or her sister, Lady Clarissa Parker, who jointly sponsored the latter's daughter, Miss Caroline Parker. Now if only Caroline lived up to their expectations . . .

Isabel licked more sticky strawberries from her fingers. "Aunt Augusta appraises every move I make."

Caroline nodded. "And Ellis skulks around, always looking like she sucks on a lemon. It is a good thing she does not rise much earlier than Aunt Augusta, or she would probably insist on accompanying us to the park." Caroline bit into another luscious tart.

"I wish I could come with you in the carriage."

"You will. Mother would rather remain in bed, but she has been a sport, rising every day and ready to leave as soon as I am. But it will not be long, Isabel, and you can come instead, just as soon as the team adjusts to the city traffic."

After Caroline helped hide the evidence of the demolished tarts in the box, Isabel carried the remains off to the kitchen by way of the back stairs.

Alone again, Caroline looked over the selection of slippers and hose, hats and gloves spread across the bed. No matter how lovely they were, they represented a duty she wished she could ignore.

The previous afternoon, Lady Longbury, dear friend of Aunt Augusta, had been escorted into the Barstow House drawing room by her son, Gilbert Cunningham, Earl of Longbury. Caroline found the young earl too tall and quite gangly, and his countenance was rather dominated by his severe overbite.

Once Aunt Augusta completed the introductions, the earl awkwardly perched on the chair beside Caroline. He grinned weakly, then gave a delicate cough and covered his mouth with a lace-trimmed handkerchief. He looked at her, then down at his hand, then over to where his mother sat.

"Have you recently arrived in town, Lord Longbury?" Caroline asked when he remained tongue-tied.

"Yes," he replied.

"We also have just come, from Berkshire." Conversation with this young fellow might be rather a chore, she feared. "Are you looking forward to the Season?"

"Indeed." His eyes were now on the teacup in his unsteady hand. Caroline reached over and took it from him, then set it on the table beside her own.

"Let us wait for a few moments for the tea to cool."

His reply was another nod of the head.

"Where is your country home?"

"In Herefordshire."

"Ah yes," Caroline replied, remembering Aunt Augusta's briefing. "You have a fine cathedral there, I believe."

"Why yes. Yes, we do."

"Please tell me about it. I have never had the good fortune to visit your region."

"The present building was begun in the eleventh century. The stained-glass windows are quite fine, but I fear the building is in need of extensive repairs."

For the next ten minutes, Caroline had only to smile, as Lord Longbury prosed on about the cathedral. How lucky, Caroline thought, she had recalled his interest in ecclesiastical architecture. He recounted the Norman origins of the building, described the ancient maps and the medieval volumes in the library, and became almost tearful as he recounted the collapse of the west tower thirty years before.

Lord Longbury sighed. "My father was dedicated to the repair of the building, and I am also devoted to the cause."

When his mother pointedly cleared her throat and glared in his direction, Lord Longbury brought his soliloquy to a close.

"I have so enjoyed talking with you, Miss Parker." He nearly tipped out of his chair. "Why, yes, and I hope you would consider accompanying me to Westminster Abbey some day. There are also fine examples of Sir Christopher Wren's work about the city."

Lady Longbury took her son's elbow, and they made their adieus to Lady Clarissa and Lady Augusta.

When the door had closed behind them, Augusta could hardly contain her delight.

"He was quite taken with you, Caroline, and he is eminently eligible. Their estate is large and has a fine old house. He has no bad habits that I can discern."

Except boring people to the utmost, Caroline thought, as well as being thoroughly drab and entirely cow-handed.

A mild morning breeze ruffled Caroline's hair as she stood on the steps of Barstow House. The trees in Berkeley Square were bathed in an aura of green and gold from the spring sun rising above the rooftops. A few houses away, two housemaids gossiped, and the laughter of one carried down the quiet street.

"Caroline," Lady Clarissa's voice came from behind the door. "Come inside this instant. Whatever are you doing standing on the doorstep like a lost caller?"

"Taking a few minutes of fresh air, Mama," Caroline replied as she stepped back inside. "The morning is lovely, but still a bit chilly. Are you sure you will be warm enough?"

Lady Clarissa pulled her fur-trimmed hat down tightly. "Remember, I am accustomed to the weather in Stockholm, where spring will not begin for a long time yet. The morning air is good for one's constitution. Very bracing indeed." She seated herself upon a tall carved chair in the foyer.

Caroline felt a rush of affection for her uncomplaining mother, who indisputably would rather be abed this and every morning. Yet she rose to attend the daily training ritual, as Caroline schooled her ponies in familiarity with both London traffic and their positions in a four-in-hand ensemble. "Mama, you know I appreciate your indulgence every morning. Very soon, I trust Isabel will accompany me."

"Do not refine upon it a moment more. I rather enjoy these times together. I am in no hurry to pronounce the ponies ready for you and Isabel."

Before the groom finished knocking, Caroline swung the door open. "Good morning, Will." She looked beyond him to the waiting rig. As usual, the team looked as elegant as one belonging to the toploftiest Corinthian on the town.

Caroline forced herself to proceed down the steps at a ladylike pace, but went immediately to the ponies' heads, cooing her good mornings and smoothing their sleek necks. Every inch of each pony had been groomed to a shining ebony finish, even to the glow of boot-blacking on hooves. Their manes were neatly braided and tails brushed to silky plumes. The soft leather and brass fittings of the harness shone brightly, and Caroline was almost disappointed Will's handiwork would find no admirers in the park.

"They look wonderful, Will." She was amused at the flush that darkened his already ruddy cheeks as he assisted Lady Clarissa into the seat.

The lead team, Oberon and Titania, was as anxious to be off as Caroline, but she took time to fuss over Puck and Ariel, giving them equal attention. A good team, whether in city or country, had to learn to stand quietly as well as respond instantly to the driver's commands.

When she had given each pony its due, Caroline settled herself beside her mother in the small phaeton used for their park visits, tucking the fur robe around their legs as shield against the crisp air.

"I declare they're the smartest four-up team I seen of any size." The groom mounted a saddle horse to follow along, a practice upon which Lady Clarissa insisted. Caroline took up the reins, and the stable boy released the ponies' heads.

She had only to speak the word, "Walk," for the team to move away from the curb and toward Hyde Park.

Other than delivery wagons and a bit of early commercial traffic, only a few equipages were on the streets. At a steady walk, the park was only minutes away.

Once on the broad drive leading through the gates, Caroline set the ponies at a rapid trot. She saw no other carriages and only an occasional rider in the distance. Even with her attention concentrated on the team, she felt the joy of open spaces in the park. Perhaps it was only her mother's scent, but Caroline was certain the hint of lilacs graced the air.

She turned the ponies off the main pathway toward the lake. They moved as smoothly as she had hoped. "What do you think of them, Mama?"

"They go very well. Better than I expected, to be honest."

"I have to admit the same thoughts." Caroline had not known just what to expect when the ponies confronted the heavy London traffic, the noise, the sooty air. After their years in the country, she feared they might be nervous and afraid, shying from every loud noise. But they seemed accustomed to light traffic after only a few days, and they behaved admirably in the quiet park. Slowly she would take them into increased traffic and watch the results.

"Caroline, are you concentrating or may I ask you about yesterday?"

Her reflection interrupted, Caroline answered, "Of course. The ponies require hardly any of my attention."

"Would I be correct in assuming you were not overly taken with your introduction to Sir Reginald Sedgewick?"

Caroline turned her thoughts to the uncomfortable scene in Lady Montgomery's drawing room the previous afternoon. Her immediate vision was of the pattern on the carpet, an intricate labyrinth of oriental vines, twisting and turning. She remembered feeling as though they clutched at her like seaweed around the legs of a bather, drawing her down and down into suffocating depths. Drowning in an ocean of polite nothingness, she barely kept herself from wrenching free and scrambling from the room. Not until many hours later had she thrown off the choking desperation that lingered.

"Lady Montgomery's taste bordered on the bizarre," Caroline responded, hoping to divert the conversation.

"I was talking about her cousin, Sir Reginald . . ."

"All that dark paneling and grinning little gargoyles."

"Really, Caroline, that is hardly a proper way to characterize a gentleman."

Caroline glanced at her mother as Lady Clarissa tried to stifle her laughter. Caroline joined in, though with a touch of ruefulness. She, after all, was the one who might be courted by the toad.

Lady Clarissa went on, still smiling. "Sir Reginald's assets are admittedly not found in his appearance, I suppose, but I thought you might be partial to his fine stable. He and your Uncle Barstow are well acquainted, though Sir Reginald is considerably younger. Did he talk with you of horses?"

"I should characterize our conversation as rather unbalanced. I asked him about his horses and he told me about his house."

"Yes, I am told he has an Elizabethan-era manor house."

Meaning cold and drafty, Caroline thought. And dark. "Then I asked him about his horses, and he told me about his three sisters who live near his estate." Not referring to their physiognomies, she assumed.

"Three unmarried sisters?" Clarissa

asked, her smile waning.

Caroline searched her memory. "I believe he said one was married, one widowed, and the other a spinster." She did remember he characterized them all as eager for him to wed. "Then I asked him about his horses and he told me what wonderful dairies operate in Lincolnshire and how all the children grow up with fine strong teeth."

"No, never say so!" Clarissa gulped between chuckles. "I am certain Augusta would not have included him if he was not both respectable and able to go about in Society. You make him sound like a . . . a . . ."

"I think gargoyle rather sums him up."

Clarissa was suddenly quite serious. "Please, dear, this is all very entertaining, but consider the advice I have offered before. An older gentleman, well-established and without bad habits, responsible in his district, respected by . . ."

"And, I believe the phrase goes, 'ready to fill up his nursery,' does it not?"

Clarissa sighed. "Perhaps so, and why not? Your children will bring you exquisite joy."

Caroline felt again on the edge of the same fathomless, smothering sensation. He probably would not talk to her of horses because in his eyes, she was little more than another broodmare.

She purposely turned the ponies in a wide arc, recovering the drive they had just left. "Mama, what you say about children seems very true. But certainly a great advantage would be an accompanying fondness for the father of those children."

"And that will come, if you look beyond the superficial to the man within."

"A gargoyle with a soul." Caroline really hoped her mother had not heard her remark.

Clarissa's silvery laughter relieved her. "I truly hope the more dignified demeanor you display for Augusta is the way you behave in company. You are too clever and too quick for your own good, my dear. Young ladies with sharp tongues do not go far."

So, Caroline thought, a few well-placed and rather stinging remarks might be a useful weapon someday.

Later that morning, Caroline shifted again on the dainty gilt chair, setting her cup to rattling on its saucer and tipping its tea to precarious angles. When their two callers left, Aunt Augusta would chastise her roundly for her twitching and lack of response to the worthy visitors. She found these conversations, centering on who was whom in the *haut ton,* whispers of waywardness in certain great houses, and where to buy the latest whimsical creations seen among the fashionable elite to be a ghastly charade.

Unlike Isabel, who scooped up every tidbit, Caroline despised the boring routine of daily calls. Worst of all were the sessions that centered upon the health of a wide variety of acquaintances and the staggering number of disorders the ladies catalogued. Caroline's estimate of the number of males involved in this whirl of chattering and tea-sipping reached a total of seven, counting yesterday's visit with Sir Reginald.

Only minutes after the ladies left, just as Aunt Augusta began asking Caroline to recite her sonnet, the butler announced Lady Elizabeth Ogden, Captain Thomas Ogden, and Mr. Simon Ogden. Caroline found herself overjoyed to see Thomas and full of curiosity about his mother.

Aunt Augusta, wiping a frown from her face, rose to embrace Lady Elizabeth. "My dear, it has been too many years," Augusta declared. "I am delighted to see you in town."

Caroline watched Thomas assess the mutual warmth of the embrace. What tales had he told his mother about his stay at Sunnyslope and Aunt Augusta's high-handed ways?

The reunion of the two ladies who had long ago shared a Season evolved into a whirl of introductions. Lady Elizabeth was supremely gracious, and Caroline found her quite lovely, looking closer to Clarissa's thirty-eight years than Augusta's buxom fifty-two.

"My son tells me you are a lady of prodigious accomplishment," Lady Elizabeth told Caroline.

Caroline felt a blush warm her cheeks, even as she demurred. "I regret to say Captain Ogden has deluded you. My meager abilities are too commonplace to deserve comment."

"Such was not his impression, I believe, Miss Parker."

Caroline was dubious about Thomas's comments, but further investigation was blocked by Aunt Augusta linking her arm through Lady Elizabeth's and beginning a discussion of who was in town.

Thomas beckoned from a corner of the room, and Caroline joined him. He looked very dashing in his dark green coat and fawn waistcoat, and she could not help a momentary twinge of jealousy as she thought of how some girl with a wealthy father would be romanced by him in the next three months.

"You are looking very fashionable today, Miss Parker." He had a distinctly devilish gleam in his eye and a slightly teasing tone in his voice.

"And you seem to be keeping the stylish tailors busy."

"All part of the crusade for you and me, is it not?"

Caroline was certain he winked. "Is the green meant to bring out your savage side? Or merely to symbolize the bucolic?"

"Lady Augusta would not approve of the barb in your tongue." He whispered as he leaned close to her ear.

She stepped away quickly and glanced at her aunt, still too involved with Lady Elizabeth to notice Caroline. Simon and Isabel were admiring a bust of Homer, or pretending to.

Thomas kept his voice low. "I have the names of three ladies my mother suggests, three Suitables. There is Miss Louisa Langham, Miss Georgina Oliver, and Miss Maria Tyler. Miss Tyler's family is in trade but marginally respectable and drowning in funds, or so it is said."

"I believe I have met Miss Langham. She seemed a quiet girl, but amiable. The next time I see her, perhaps I can engage her in conversation. What would you like to know about her?"

Thomas assumed a sardonic grin. "You mean beyond the size of her portion? I suppose it would be nice to know if she has a sense of humor."

"I shall endeavor to make the acquaintance of Miss Oliver and Miss Tyler."

He nodded, though he looked anything but cheery. "Thank you. Tell me how the ponies are going."

"First, just what did you tell your mother about me? You did not exaggerate my pitiful ability at the pianoforte, did you? Or tell her I can sing? If such tales get around, some gathering of the *ton* might have a very disagreeable evening, at my expense."

Thomas grinned and shook his head. "I told her you were a famous pony trainer."

Caroline gasped.

"And you will be making your debut at Astley's Royal Circus before the Season is out."

"Oh, you did not!" No one in her entire lifetime had such a capacity to needle her.

But when she looked into his eyes, they had turned to a velvety blue that made her knees weak and her hands tremble.

"You really do look quite lovely, Miss Parker."

Her heart drummed so loudly she was certain he could hear its thump.

"You do the ladies of your household credit." He drew a single finger across the lace mitt on her hand, and she grasped the back of a chair with the other. Her limbs were in danger of failing to support her, as she struggled to regain her composure.

"Why, Captain Ogden, such taradiddle. I am afraid you will have to polish that performance considerably before you try it on the Suitables. If not, even with my help, you will never succeed." Caroline was sure he knew she was prevaricating, but if she did not stop his advances, she feared she would tumble into his arms in this very drawing room in front of Aunt Augusta and both of their mamas.

But he leaned even closer and covered her hand with his. "I am nothing if not sincere, Caroline. You will be a great success, and I fear I shall envy the fellows who please you."

Caroline felt herself shiver and dared to

look into his eyes only briefly. Her disquiet was exquisite.

"In fact, I shall sit in the first row at Astley's to cheer you on!"

Caroline felt her tension dwindle in an instant. "You, sir, are impertinent, and I have a notion to report that to your mother."

Thomas laughed, moving to the window, a safe distance away. "Before you do, I have a savory item of gossip to relate."

"Anything but that," Caroline moaned. "I've heard so much boring gossip, I've had my fill."

"But this little *on dit* concerns you."

"In that case, proceed at once!"

"In White's last evening, I overheard Lord Dunwood talking about two beautiful ladies driving four ponies in Hyde Park that morning. He was most anxious to learn their names."

Caroline cringed. "You did not tell him?"

"No, indeed. The mystery will add to your allure."

"But there's hardly anyone in the park that early. How could he have seen us?"

"I don't know, but you will not have much privacy as the story spreads." Thomas shrugged.

"Do you mean someone might come looking for us?"

"Indeed, I predict more than one will venture forth."

Caroline did not know whether to feel flattered or annoyed. For now, she would have to make her training exercises even earlier, at least until the team was ready for public inspection. Poor Mama would lose another hour or two of her beauty sleep. "I wish it had not happened so soon, but it is not to be helped."

He shrugged again, with a most cultivated nonchalance.

When Lady Elizabeth, Captain Ogden, and Simon took their leave, Caro was pleased to hear Aunt Augusta invite them to a quiet dinner, *en famille,* as she called it, to be held the next evening.

Upon arising the next day, Caroline took Isabel aside before more callers arrived and again warned her cousin against letting anyone know of her arrangement with Thomas.

Isabel nodded her auburn-curled head. "Do not fret, Caro. I am looking at this Season in a very selfish way indeed. If you are a Toast and Aunt Augusta is pleased, perhaps she will sponsor me next year. I cannot imagine my mama

184

making a go of it, can you?"

Just the thought of Aunt Letitia coping with the intricate details of preparing for the Season, much less making a splash in Society, made Caroline giggle.

Isabel went on. "You and Captain Ogden have a clever deal. Spying on the Eligibles and the Suitables is perfect."

"Spying is not exactly what I'd call it." More like fighting for survival, Caroline thought.

Lady Elizabeth hurried into her son's rooms, brushing his man aside in her haste. At the door of the library, she paused, discomfited by the poorly dressed man who sat across the desk from Thomas. When he stood, his hands pressed on the table, she could not help staring. He had only one leg.

"Good afternoon, Mother. May I present Mr. Joshua Deeble, a friend of mine from the peninsula. Josh, my mother, Lady Elizabeth Ogden." Concluding the introductions, he sat back to watch their reactions.

Lady Elizabeth quickly recovered her characteristic grace. "Mr. Deeble, I am pleased to know you. Although Thomas has declined to give me many of the details, I am certain that all of you deserve our heartfelt thanks for your brave service."

Josh seemed momentarily tongue-tied.

"But, please," Lady Elizabeth continued, "let us not dwell on the unpleasant past. Thomas says you have news of Aldonhurst."

"Took a likin' to the old lord, I did."

Thomas poured his mother a glass of wine and refilled Josh's. "Figured you would. He is full of fascinating stories when he is clearheaded."

"But he ain't got much grip on reality. Mrs. Stippick is taking good care of him. When she don't come, he plum forgets to eat. But I took down what I could. A whole portfolio full." He gestured to a folder of papers on the desk.

"What can be salvaged of the house?"

"Needs a fair amount a' work, I'd say. Roof leaks, probably has for decades. Good bit of rot. At best, I'd say it ain't going to collapse for a few more years."

"Comforting," Thomas murmured. "Go on."

"The estate is in bad condition. The bailiff was a cheat and once I started asking questions, he disappeared. Several of the tenant farms are empty. Most of the remaining tenants are demoralized and don't do much productive."

Thomas nodded. "As I assumed."

"Clearly the bailiff pocketed all the money for improvements. Houses of tenants falling down. That scoundrel was to blame, 'n maybe he's even more than a scoundrel. I think he fouled a well on one place. Acres of pastureland are overgrazed and support fewer and fewer livestock. It makes a man cry to see such waste, Captain. Land fallow, great empty hills with at least two abandoned alum mines, and no work in the village, neither."

Without substantial funds, Thomas figured, what could he do to rebuild a whole way of life there? But Josh was not finished.

"So, Captain, there was a house here in town. In St. James Place, I reckon. Couldn't find records of sale or lease, but the old marquess told me about the place. Do you figure it could have been shut up for twenty years?"

"A house?" Elizabeth chimed in. "Why yes, now that you say so, I remember Thomas's father pointing it out when we were newly married. Surely it has not been closed that long."

Thomas ran his fingers through his hair.

"I will investigate, starting first thing tomorrow morning. Just one more thing requiring ample repairs, I suppose."

"I never got to the old account books, more 'n ten years ago. Had enough trouble trying to make out what's been done lately. Course there's just a trickle of income nowadays and it don't go far."

"What would you do if the place was yours, Josh?"

"Get to work 'n plan on spendin' a lifetime. Pray t' find buried treasure. But it's a far grander place than I'd try 'n farm."

"Don't give me that! You never were destined to farm, Josh, with two legs or three. If that was your aim, why spend all those years in school learning mathematics?"

"Maybe just reaching a bit beyond myself," Josh muttered.

"How about taking on the job that cursed bailiff botched and count on spending that lifetime there? Keep your eye on Lord Aldonhurst at the same time. Set up the best house on the property for your family. Think about what the main house needs. Perhaps you might jot down some ideas for me and estimate the costs. Report back to me in four weeks."

Both Josh and Lady Elizabeth were left

speechless, Josh nodding in gratitude and Thomas's mother shaking her head in surprise and pride.

Nine

"The lines of your gown are perfect." Lady Clarissa watched her daughter enter the drawing room of Barstow House. "You look charming."

"I am glad you approve," Caroline murmured, giving her mother a little hug. The high-waisted white dress with its rosettes and ribbons of soft peach was one of her favorites.

"Yes," Aunt Augusta agreed. "Very becoming and easy to change the trimming color. You can wear it many times."

Caroline dared not look her mother in the eye again. Oh, that penny-pinching Augusta! Fortunately Isabel was still upstairs, redoing her hair for the third time. Otherwise, all three of them would have erupted in gales of laughter. By staring intently at the toe of her white silken slipper, she was able to let the moment pass without even a giggle.

This evening was the first of what Augusta called her little dinners *en famille,* modest events, she said, to introduce

Caroline to particularly eligible prospects and their families. Until Captain Ogden and his mother were invited to attend, Caroline had been dreading the evening. Now she looked forward to seeing Thomas assess one Eligible firsthand. Even so, meeting the third of Aunt Augusta's original list of Eligibles, and thus a prime candidate to become her husband, gave Caroline the shudders. Neither Lord Longbury nor Sir Reginald caused her a particularly affirmative feeling toward courtship, much less marriage.

"Caroline, you will play for us after dinner," Augusta declared. "Preferably without stumbling, or forgetting —"

"You'll do beautifully," Clarissa interrupted.

Amazing to think they are sisters, Caroline mused as she watched her mother and Aunt Augusta seat themselves. They hardly resembled each other in disposition, attitude or appearance. Augusta's ample proportions were the exact opposite of Clarissa's petite daintiness. Like her daughter, Clarissa preferred simplicity in her wardrobe, a minimum of furbelows and flounces, fringes and tassels. Clarissa, in gauzy lavender-blue embroidered muslin, wore simple pearl bracelets and a modest gold locket, flawless in their classical restraint. Augusta, on the other hand, ornamented her substantial dimensions with elaborate draperies of cerise satin and multiple strings of shimmering beads. Her matching turban, sparkling with sequins, winked like some maritime beacon each time she moved her head.

Just as Isabel appeared, the butler entered. "Lady Poynton and Lord Graham," he announced.

As they went through the flurry of introductions, Caroline was surprised to find Charles Graham a decidedly attractive gentleman. His evening clothes were correct to a fault and his dark hair was arranged perfectly a la Brutus. He was particularly obsequious to Aunt Augusta and exhibited a dashing charm to her mother.

"*Enchanté*, Miss Parker." He bent over Caroline's hand.

"Very pleased to meet you," she responded. To her own ears her voice sounded rather like a croak.

When Lord Graham returned to his mother's side to escort her to a chair, Caroline caught Isabel's eye. Her cousin's smile of greeting was so wide Caroline feared Isabel's face might split.

"A distinct improvement," Caroline whispered.

"That he is," Isabel sighed, as though half in love with him already.

When they were seated, Caroline tried to ignore the frank appraisal in Lady Poynton's eyes. She busied herself with rearranging her skirts, but when she looked up again, the haughty baroness was peering through her lorgnette directly into Caroline's face.

Lady Poynton's sharp voice shrilled in the quiet room. "She has a pleasing look, just as you reported, Augusta. Quite as pretty as her mother." She spoke as if neither Caroline nor Clarissa were present. "She will have to be, of course, if she wants to hold Charles's attention."

Charles had the grace to move his chair closer to Caroline's and speak in a quiet voice. "Please excuse the *mater*, Miss Parker. She utters every transitory thought that flits through her mind. I beg you, don't be insulted."

Caroline smiled, raising her eyes to his. "I promise not to take offense. I assure you she is far from the only lady of the *ton* who seems to believe we green girls are afflicted with defective hearing."

"You don't say. Well, now that is a bit of consolation."

"Lady Elizabeth and Captain Ogden," the butler intoned.

In the midst of another round of introductions, bows and handshakes, Thomas cast a wink in Caroline's direction. He seated himself next to Lady Poynton with only a hint of a grimace. Though she had no idea what he was actually saying, Caroline could imagine him charming the baroness's sour expression into a smile, to enlist her as an unconscious ally in his quest. He was obviously using his most amiable manner this evening. His rakish grin had a predictable effect on Lady Poynton, who was soon fluttering her fan and even gushing a girlish giggle at something he whispered in her ear.

Augusta's brief but calculated cough brought Caroline's attention back to her side of the room and the realization that Lord Graham had been speaking. She caught something about the Princess of Wales.

Isabel was rapt. "Are she and the Prince fighting again?" she asked.

"Shush." Caroline noted her aunt's frown. "Aunt Augusta will send you from the room if she hears you talk of such things."

"What was that, Miss Parker?" Lord Graham asked.

Caroline turned to him with her widest smile. "Oh, nothing of import. Please do go on with your story."

He lowered his voice. "I note the storm clouds gathering on your worthy aunt's brow. No doubt she is concerned for the seemliness of our conversation. One assumes Byron is an even less suitable subject?"

Caroline's smile grew progressively more genuine. "Your discernment of our quandary is perceptive indeed. The more our aunt warns us off a topic, the more we wish to discover, and the more suspicious she becomes."

"Then perhaps you would join me for a stroll in the park one of these fine days? I would be delighted to escort you and Lady Isabel in a turn or two around the latest *on dits*. As the Season gets under way, the clever gossip whirls faster and faster through Society, and one hates to miss a single delicious item."

Caroline felt Isabel's enthusiasm radiating from her smile. "I would be pleased to join you, Lord Graham, but of course I cannot vouch for Isabel's interest," Caroline teased.

As the party rose to go to the dining room, Caroline purposely left Isabel to

Lord Graham's attention.

Captain Ogden offered one arm to Lady Poynton and the other to Aunt Augusta, nearly putting Caroline into a fit of laughter. He appeared so very proper and dignified, yet she could imagine what he was thinking as he guided the two ladies, one quite plump and the other all bones and angles. She hoped she would hear his commentary on the scene a bit later.

Between them, the two gentlemen kept the dinner conversation flowing in a lively manner, an amicable competition to exceed each other in charm and propriety. Lady Poynton divided her time between her continued inspection of Caroline and resolute statements of her views on whatever topic happened to catch her fancy. When Aunt Augusta led the ladies back to the drawing room, both Captain Ogden and Lord Graham declared an aversion to losing their company and decided to forego their port.

Without quite knowing how she got there, Caroline found herself at the pianoforte, with Lord Graham gallantly offering to turn the pages for her.

"That would be very nice of you," she responded, but she soon had second thoughts. Lord Graham was too smooth by half, she reflected as she began to play. And she strongly suspected he was actually peering at her bosom when he leaned over to reach the music. Was not all of this just too, too contrived? An evening of forced gaiety, when that auction ring at Tattersall's would have been the more honest venue. Parade out the filly for everyone's scrutiny and start the bidding.

Caroline glanced at Thomas Ogden, who was standing across the room speaking with Lady Poynton and Isabel but keeping his eye on her. Again, she was certain she saw him give a little wink.

Caroline hardly paid attention to how well or how poorly she played, but contrarily, her fingers were particularly supple and artful. Lord Graham turned another page. He was simply too fawning, too attentive.

After three pieces, she gave her place at the keyboard to her mother, leaving Lord Graham to assist. Caroline wished she could talk with Thomas, get his view on Lord Graham, but he was quite completely engaged by the baroness, who tapped him rhythmically on the arm as she went on.

Lady Elizabeth beckoned to Caroline, gesturing to the chair beside her. "You play very nicely, Miss Parker."

"Thank you, but I am afraid my repertoire is rather limited."

Thomas's mother had a smile as wide and open as her son's. "No one will remember what you play from evening to evening, dear. Three or four masterpieces will do you well. My son tells me you are a young lady of particularly refined tastes."

Caroline looked at her in surprise. Was this another of Thomas's jokes? "Oh, I have very little to boast of in the way of refinement." Nor could she boast of a sizable dowry, and she was certain Thomas's mother knew so.

"I do not believe my son shares that opinion. We are hoping you will join us in a little excursion tomorrow afternoon. I have already discussed this with your mother and received her permission. I presume you will agree?"

"An excursion?"

"Only a brief time, Miss Parker — a trifling matter, really, having to do with household decor, shall we say?"

Caroline was mystified, but saw no reason to decline. "I shall be pleased to join you."

As the guests took their leave, Caroline expected some words of explanation from Thomas, but he correctly bowed his good-bye and left. Just the devilish hint of a twinkle in his eye belied his graceful manner. Whatever was he up to?

The next morning, Caroline had no sooner driven the ponies through the gate in Hyde Park than a half dozen riders saluted her, their horses jostling one another as they jockeyed for position beside the carriage.

She smiled and waved, but neither slowed nor stopped. What the ponies needed was a steady hand. The ponies tossed their heads but did not shy, though they clearly were growing nervous as horses skirted their path and the riders offered loud greetings.

Lady Clarissa sighed. "I have been expecting this. Captain Ogden warned me that our change to even earlier hours had been found out."

Caroline leaned close and whispered to her mother. "Now that we are discovered for good, we can sleep later and bring the ponies at a reasonable hour."

"I am delighted to hear it."

Ariel seemed to be the only pony indicating his displeasure by shaking his head, switching his tail wildly and crowding a little toward Puck. Generally, Caroline was pleased at the mildness of their reaction to the proximity of so many horses.

The dew still shone on the grass. The trees were more than hinting at green, and the willows near the water were already glowing in pale yellow-green. In contrast, the riders wore coats of many colors, from bright yellow to an intense turquoise. To Caroline's eye, they rather spoiled the view.

At the top of the rise, she pulled the ponies to a walk. Immediately several gentlemen thrust one another aside for the right to be first to greet Lady Clarissa and Caroline. The resulting melee left them both laughing, and Caroline urged the ponies onward at a smart walk to keep them from being entangled in the fracas.

At last the horses sorted themselves out, without much help from their riders that Caroline could determine, but the ponies had clearly had enough commotion. She could feel their tension and kept a tight hold on the lead team. What she needed was space to turn them and escape the pack of riders. As she concentrated on the team, she barely heard the multitudinous praise and tributes to their excellence. Miss Parker's abilities were declared stellar, and Lady Clarissa was abundantly clever to have a daughter with such talent.

Caroline waved them away. "Please, gentlemen, give the poor ponies a bit of space. They are unused to close company."

"But, I say . . ." Lord Longbury began, and they all began to talk at once. Immediately the ponies' nervous stamping and restless footwork grew.

"Back off," a familiar voice called, with an air of authority that seemed to impress the throng. "Form up behind the carriage and keep well back."

Caroline turned to see Thomas Ogden herding the others to a neat formation in her phaeton's wake. He rode his tall rangy bay, a mount with the fearless action of an experienced battlefield veteran.

Lady Clarissa waved to him. "I think Captain Ogden has appeared just in time."

Caroline soothed the ponies and, given more space, they quickly settled down to a steady pace. "Yes, about one more rambunctious rider would have set them off, I am afraid. We have a way to go before they are ready for such an abundance of traffic."

Now, as they trotted along with the parade of riders in their wake, Caroline found herself struggling to remember some of the more ludicrous comments to share with Isabel, such as the paean to the shine of the ponies' hooves, the ode to Miss Parker's dainty grip on the ribbons, and others, each more nonsensical than the last.

They were accompanied all the way around Hyde Park and back to the mews by no less than half a dozen riders, all of whom pledged to be at Miss Parker's service the very next morning or at any time she chose to drive out.

"I truly thank you. As you could see, we need to move slowly introducing the team to crowded paths. If Captain Ogden had not come along when he did, I fear my darlings would have tried to run away," she explained.

The fellow in the yellow coat nodded vigorously. "And I was nearly a miscreant myself. Don't believe I realized the peril in our jumbling about. You can be sure, Miss Parker, that I will be more cautious in the future."

"That goes for me," another rider said. "I shall be looking forward to being with you in the morning, on patrol, as they say."

"Well, no harm done today, and I am sure the team will make quick progress, should we have company again." Caroline spoke resignedly.

Thomas Ogden sat his bay calmly,

waiting for the others to depart. When Caroline was finally free, he swung down and stood beside her. "What a squadron of useless fops. Not much brain matter in any of them, I fear."

"You were a great help, Captain Ogden. I am much indebted to you."

"And I will join you each morning for a while, until the team is accustomed to company, though I might suggest a later hour."

Lady Clarissa joined them on the cobblestones. "Thank you, Captain Ogden. You will receive no dissent from me. You truly may have saved us from a dire mishap."

Thomas smiled. "I think your daughter's skill was the deciding factor."

Caroline felt herself blush as he complimented her. "Would you come in for coffee?"

"Thank you, not this morning. I have several things to do, I am afraid, before we come for you later."

"Where are we going? You never explained."

"I will tell you all about it. For now, let it suffice to say we have discovered a new puzzle to unsnarl."

"Until then," she said, as he remounted his horse.

In the breakfast room, Caroline dropped into a chair with a sigh. "At least that is over now."

"Yes, and I am proud of you, my dear." Clarissa poured a cup of coffee for herself. "You were all that is proper and polite. You did not encourage their attentions; neither did you refuse to acknowledge their accolades. You controlled the team very well."

"I credit Oberon and Titania. As the lead pair, they were most in jeopardy of being trampled and they behaved almost perfectly. Once the riders stopped milling around in front of them, the team was fine."

"We really must thank Captain Ogden again. He was both efficient and rather gallant, I thought."

Caroline's cheeks were still warm. Despite his teasing manner, he was there when she most needed him. "I am very glad he arrived when he did."

"I am sure that was no accident!"

Caroline helped herself at the sideboard. "I think the less said to Aunt Augusta, the better."

Clarissa smiled at her daughter. "Agreed. However, she is bound to hear of our encounter."

"But if we do not refine upon it, why should she?"

"Augusta is concerned about your reputation."

"I do not see anything fast or loose about driving my own team in early morning."

"Of course your activities are above reproach. But Augusta would rather have your status among the *ton* be that of lovely and accomplished young lady."

Witless and vacant, Caroline thought, but voiced accord with her mother.

Caroline stood in awe at the size of the house, fully five windows wide on the first story. No knocker was fitted to the front door, a sure sign no one was in residence.

Caroline was flattered to be included in the first visit to Aldon House, every bit as eager to see what would unfold as Thomas and Lady Elizabeth.

Thomas gazed at the size of the mansion with a half smile. "Who knows if this is going to be an asset or simply another drain on my finances?"

Lady Elizabeth patted his arm. "I pray it will be the former, Thomas."

Josh fit an old iron key into the lock, and the door opened on well-oiled hinges. The foyer was dark, the chandelier draped in a white cover, as were the chairs placed between the closed doors. A graceful stairway curved into the gloom above.

Lady Elizabeth took candles from her reticule and passed them to the others. Caroline peeked through the door on the left and discovered a well-proportioned room with all the furniture pushed together in the middle and draped in Holland covers against the dust. Flinging open the shutters, she saw a parquet floor and walls lined in silk. Dust motes danced in the unaccustomed sunlight.

Lady Elizabeth lifted the edge of the covering for a look at the furniture, but as she folded it back, there was a loud hissing that made her jump in surprise.

A cat leaped out of the chair and fled the room.

Lady Elizabeth dropped the cover. "A cat! How could an animal survive in here alone for all these years?"

Thomas placed an arm around his mother's shoulders. "There must be someone around. Let's try the kitchen."

They found the door to the servant's stairs and called out a greeting. Hearing no answer, they went down into the basement rooms, checking each until they came to the kitchen. Clearly someone lived here, although no one was in evidence.

Thomas called out again. "Hello! Anybody here?"

Puzzled, Caroline let herself out the rear entrance. A small garden was laid out between the edge of the brick courtyard and a high hedge. Peeking over a gate, she could see the remnants of a formal garden, now overgrown but bright with budding branches and a scraggly patch of primroses.

Thomas followed her. "It must have been beautiful once. But who in the devil lives in that kitchen?"

Josh came out of the stable beyond the courtyard. "Other 'n dirt, there ain't a sign of nuthin'."

Caroline examined the tiny garden near the door. "Someone has been planting this little plot."

At that moment, the rear gate opened and a bent figure entered, a shawl over her head and a basket on her arm. When she looked up to see the four intruders, she stopped and stared. "Mornin'."

Lady Elizabeth took a step forward. "Why, good morning. Are you in the employ of the Marquess of Aldonhurst?"

The elderly woman gave a little curtsy.

"Indeed I am. Though many years it's been since I seen his lordship."

"Are there other servants here?"

"Ah, no 'm, all else has left, so it's jes' me alone. And kin I be askin' who you be?"

"I am Lady Elizabeth Ogden. The marquess has asked my son, Mr. Ogden, and his bailiff, Mr. Deeble, to look out for his affairs for a time."

The old woman's sharp eyes moved back and forth from one to another. "He is well, then? I was just a girl when I came here, and then I thought he was old. But I never heared that he'd turned up his toes."

Lady Elizabeth smiled. "He is well, but very frail. Now how can we help you with these things?"

In the kitchen, Thomas showed Brigid, the housekeeper, his note from the marquess.

She squinted at the cramped script. "I cain't make out much of it, but I see the seal. That's good enough for me."

Caroline and the others listened with fascination to Brigid tell how she gradually had assumed more and more responsibilities. Over the years, one by one, the other servants left for new posts when the marquess began to miss transfers of funds for the salaries. She had survived here, it turned out, by selling a number of items the departing servants left behind and occasionally pawning a few small things belonging to the marquess.

Thomas commended her for her ability to keep the house in good shape. "When I report to the marquess, I will tell him of your faithfulness to your duties."

She looked down at her gnarled hands. "Quite a loverly silver tea set went to fix the roof a year ago. And the garden's gone to wrack and ruin."

"Quite understandable in the circumstances. Mr. Deeble and I found that the solicitor who once took care of Aldonhurst's city business died a decade ago."

She nodded. "I figured old Mr. Condon musta' passed."

Lady Elizabeth was anxious to see the upstairs. "If it is in reasonable condition, we might open it up for lease in a few weeks."

Caroline left Thomas and Lady Elizabeth on the first floor, examining the furniture in the drawing room. She went up another flight of stairs and into a room at the back of the house. Again, everything was cloaked in dusty sheets, and the heavy brocade hangings on a canopied bed were closed. A stale smell of neglect permeated the air as she walked around the room. On the dressing table, she found a glass jar of dried rose petals, and when she opened and stirred the contents, the sweet fragrance began to chase the mustiness away.

"What do you think?" Thomas's voice startled her.

"The house is beautiful, aside from needing a regiment of maids to dust and sweep." Caroline walked to the window, held the drapery aside, and looked down at the garden below.

Thomas came to stand beside her. "Everything needs trimming down there, if not replacement. It's nothing but a tangle."

"I think I can see a pattern. It looks like a small medieval knot garden."

He looked at her in surprise, bringing a blush to her cheeks. "A knot garden? Whatever is that?"

"A love knot." She felt suddenly embarrassed. "Just a design."

"What kind of design?"

She looked away and did not answer. In vain she tried to think of another topic, but he was standing too close. He made her feel befuddled.

"Come now, Miss Parker, please tell me. What is a love knot?"

"You already think I have nothing in my head but nonsensical notions about one and only one concern."

"Referring to the subject of love? And now that subject has become nonsensical?"

Though his voice was teasing and light-hearted, she felt uncomfortable. "Captain Ogden, I find your insinuations nonsensical. That is all. And if you really want to know, which I sincerely doubt, a love knot is a pattern of planting in intertwined circles, representing the unbroken bonds of true love. And the design is often executed in hedges of the herbs which represent everlasting and eternal sentiments. Not that you believe in such things." By the end of her soliloquy, she could feel her cheeks flaming.

"Miss Parker, you are especially beautiful when your dander is raised."

She felt a spark of real anger. "You delight in teasing me. I do not find it pleasing to be treated so."

"Then let me apologize. I was only jesting." His voice grew husky, and her heart pounded faster and faster. "Forgive me?"

He caught her hand and raised it to his lips. "I know that none of the Eligibles would treat you in such a rag-mannered fashion."

She could not suppress a little gasp of laughter. "None of the Eligibles has the slightest urge to tease, I am afraid."

"Afraid?" He caressed her hand gently. "I thought you did not care for teasing."

"Oh, you know what I mean. They do not laugh at much of anything. Lord Longbury proses on and on about carved choirs, Lord Graham wants to gossip about Prinny, and Sir Reginald merely harrumphs."

Thomas raised her hand to his lips. "My poor Miss Parker, how dull it must be."

His warm breath on her fingers and the softness of his lips made her tremble.

She tried to pull away. "You have not told me what you think of any of them yet."

He gave a rueful laugh and stepped away. "Longbury is a rich fool, Sedgewick is an old fool, and Graham is the worst of all. In dun territory, I hear."

"But the Poyntons are well set, are they not? Do not tell me Aunt Augusta could be mistaken!"

"Graham's family money is fortunately well protected from his gambling debts. Certainly his mother knows his predicament, but has her own schemes. The old bat insists he acquire a wife and sire children. Then she might see to his funds, but not until."

"I cannot imagine why she thinks I might be a prospect."

He came back to her side and looked into her eyes. "To be honest, you are pretty enough to attract his attention, and your small dowry is not enough to remove him from her control, which is exactly what she is looking for."

Caroline's voice shook. "I play the role of pawn."

"And don't forget, of broodmare." He dropped his voice to a whisper and leaned closer.

"Hah!" Her protest died in the hypnotic sight of his lips nearing hers.

Caroline swayed toward him as he wrapped her in his arms. For just a moment she would let herself taste this forbidden honey of his lips, feel his perilous caress. But again he quickly drew away.

"Caroline, you make me forget myself!" He turned and headed for the stairs.

She stood with her eyes closed, enveloped in the delicate scent of roses, reveling in the delightful new sensations that vibrated within her whole body. Life was becoming very complicated indeed.

Ten

Caroline snuggled into her pillow, then rolled over and stretched. Slowly she opened her eyes. Heavens above, it was full daylight, far later than her usual dawn awakening. Memories crowded into her consciousness, and she smiled, pulling the coverlet up to her chin. The ponies would have to wait today. She needed some time to savor her little success at the Queen's drawing room. Only yesterday she had nervously rehearsed in that outlandish outfit, feeling like the silliest of green schoolroom chits. Now she knew every other girl felt the same way about their curtsy to the Queen, and not a one of them had so much as strained the bounds of perfect propriety. All their fears had been foolish.

Caroline stretched again and giggled into the covers. Yesterday, her mother said, was the most terrifying of the events she would have to face in the coming weeks: attending the Court's drawing room and being presented to the Queen. After all the fussing and waiting and crush outside, she found the actual reception quite anti-climactic. First there had been the ordeal of acquiring and learning to walk in the Court dress outfit, a hoop-skirted remnant of the previous century. She looked entirely ridiculous in the looking glass, and the skirt felt incredibly unwieldy when she tried to walk. But after much practicing and curtsying before Aunt Augusta, she finally bowed before Queen Charlotte and her daughters without falling on her face. The Queen was actually rather old-fashioned looking herself, Caroline had observed, as were the princesses. Caroline hardly said a word, since all of them spoke with Augusta and Clarissa as honored old friends.

Her thoughts interrupted by scratching at the door, she called, "Enter."

"I cannot wait to hear every detail," her cousin bubbled.

Caroline assumed an imperious tone. "First of all, Miss Isabel, you should be informed that Lady Augusta Stolper is indeed an acquaintance of Her Majesty Queen Charlotte."

"She was not gammoning us, then?"

"Apparently not. Of course, my mother was known to the Queen also. Once I had been presented, I did nothing but watch the others. It looked rather like a sea of bobbing ostrich feathers."

"But was it not exciting, Caro?"

"Once I got past the curtsy without falling over in a dead faint, I found it quite dull. Aunt Augusta and Mama towed me around, introducing me to people they knew, and I stood by while they chatted. Unless I am vastly mistaken, there was not one man in attendance under age forty. I am heartily glad the whole affair is over."

"This very moment Aunt Augusta is packing your dress away. She wants to be sure I can wear it next year!"

Caroline joined Isabel in hearty laughter. "Our dear aunt is taking a hint from royalty. Some of the dresses the Princesses wore looked at least a decade old."

"How gauche! Now we can concentrate on your ball, Caroline."

Caroline sighed. "The best thing about that occasion will be the arrival of your parents with Becky and Henry. I miss those little demons."

"Pooh. I have not missed them for a moment. Now tell me which gentleman will have the first dance with you?"

A frown clouded Caroline's face. "There's the rub, indeed. Captain Ogden's reports about the Eligibles are sadly discouraging."

"Then you must find some new prospects."

Caroline grimaced. "How utterly exasperating. Would you ring for Peg, please, Isabel? I might as well face the day."

Thomas admired his cravat in the glass, silently congratulating himself on how well he looked. He was ready earlier than usual tonight, though not too early to call upon his mother, who would probably be delighted to share an aperitif with him before attending Miss Parker's presentation ball. Before he headed out the door, he grabbed his walking stick. As much as he would like to do without it tonight, he dared not risk a setback now that full strength and feeling were returning at last.

Caroline's ball was the first of many such affairs in the coming months, one he and Caroline had carefully discussed. In his mind, Thomas ran over his prodigious set of responsibilities as he walked the short distance to Pemstead House. Naturally the Eligibles would be in attendance, and one of his assignments was to talk with each and take their measure. Then he was to dance at least once with each of the

Suitables, the three young ladies his mother favored and Caroline had invited. To humor his mother, he would be careful to remember the names of any more candidates she might put forward by suggesting he lead one out for a turn on the dance floor.

Of course, Thomas mused, Caroline could not scrutinize the Suitables tonight. As the center of attention, she would no doubt be claimed for dances by her uncles, cousins, and close family friends. His final assignment, however, the one he particularly looked forward to, was to step in if Caroline lacked a partner for any set. In fact, the august Augusta herself had assigned him that rather pleasant duty.

Lady Elizabeth met him with a wide smile.

He made a deep bow. "You look barely beyond debut age yourself."

"Oh, la, Thomas. You are a sad flirt." She made a little twirl away from him.

"And you, Mother dear, are destined to break hearts this Season, or I miss my guess."

Before they finished more than half a glass of wine, the butler announced the arrival of the Pemstead town coach with the viscount's crest upon its shiny doors.

"Why, Mother, you never stop surprising me."

Head high and with a conspiratorial smile, Lady Elizabeth sniffed. "Certainly you did not expect me to go about in a common hack, Thomas. Your brother hardly needs his coach if he is not in town."

His only response was a hearty laugh.

When the luxurious coach arrived at the door of Barstow House, the traffic seemed particularly intense, and the wait longer both outside and in the foyer than either Thomas or Lady Elizabeth expected.

"Apparently," Lady Elizabeth whispered, "there must be a very important gathering later in the evening for the crush here to be so heavy this early."

Thomas agreed. He saw a number of his acquaintances ahead in the crowd, including two dukes and the heirs to several important estates.

To his surprise, Mr. Nicholas Martin joined him and greeted his mother. As a close friend and schoolmate of Lady Elizabeth's oldest son, Viscount Pemstead, Nicholas knew her well. Thomas listened to the two of them discussing the health and well-being of Lionel and his family as well as Mr. Martin's mother, Countess

Graverson, who would arrive in town shortly. Then Thomas almost laughed out loud when Nicholas directed a question to him.

"Have you met Miss Parker yet? I hear she commands particular admiration this year. Everyone seems quite taken with her handsome team of four black ponies."

"Yes, I have been so privileged. In fact, on a recent visit to her uncle's estate, I had the pleasure of riding with the team."

"The devil you say, Ogden — beg pardon, Lady Elizabeth. Quite a pretty miss, and judging from the crush, she'll be all the rage this year."

Thomas warned himself not to take umbrage. He ought to be pleased and proud for Caroline, not irritated. "Yes, I believe she will be a Toast."

As they edged into the house, Thomas caught the sense of excitement that graced only a few of the balls in any Season, a sense of building enthusiasm and imminent acclamation. No one could precisely predict when this unspoken mutual accord would occur, but Thomas was willing to bet every ha'penny of his dwindling purse that by tomorrow London would hail Miss Parker as this year's Incomparable. All around him, Thomas heard nothing but superlatives about the occasion's honoree — her beauty, her appealing smile, her sweet nature. The more he heard, the less he approved. Caroline was having her triumph. His job would be easy: to sort through a gaggle of suitors to find the most tolerable one. The thought gave him no comfort at all.

When he finally reached the Earl and Countess of Barstow, his sisters Lady Augusta and Lady Clarissa, and Miss Parker, Thomas fought off his aggravation. The family greeted him with affection, and Lady Augusta warmly embraced Lady Elizabeth.

Thomas caught Caroline's eye and gave her a special smile and nod, then backed away as Nicholas began to address her.

Caroline looked a vision. Her white dress sparkled with twinkling gilt accents and white roses crowned her golden hair. Instead of just another miss in white, Thomas thought she appeared an angel. He could not turn his eyes away.

"Captain Ogden, do you have windmills in your head?" Isabel asked from right beside him.

Thomas shook off his dreamy trance. "Good evening, Lady Isabel. You are looking very lovely tonight."

"Do not look so surprised to see me. Aunt Augusta objected strongly, but I am just as stubborn as she is."

"Then would a dance be in order?"

"Please. Since I am here, I intend to enjoy myself."

Promising Isabel the third set, Thomas accompanied his mother into the ballroom.

"Seems to be a perfect crush," Lady Elizabeth remarked and Thomas nodded, wondering why he felt no joy in the evidence that his share of the bargain with Caroline would be effortless.

After partnering his mother in the first set, Thomas found Miss Langham, who looked surprised to be sought out, though she said hardly a word. When he returned her to her mother, he was surprised to find Lord Longbury waiting with Lady Langham. Perhaps, Thomas thought, Gaunt Gilbert was hankering after an addition to his ample fortune. Don't be a sourpuss, Thomas cautioned himself, as he set off to find Lady Isabel.

After his fifth straight set, Thomas found a secluded corner and leaned against a marble column. The elegant rooms of Barstow House were brilliantly lit by imposing crystal-hung candelabra. Thomas noticed the orchestra played none of the newer dances, but the revelers did not mind. Amid banks of ferns and cascades of white roses, Thomas watched the smiling faces, fluttering fans, and graceful flowing gowns of the young ladies. Even in this splendid company, Caroline glowed with conspicuous supremacy over the others. Her features had the perfect degree of animation, her gestures a flawless refinement, and he simply stood and observed her dancing set after set, his duties temporarily forgotten.

When the music stopped, Thomas quickly broke out of his reverie, noting Charles Graham escorting Miss Parker in to dinner. Thomas decided then and there that Graham would have to be eliminated from the Eligibles. Graham's smile as he gazed into Caroline's eyes resembled nothing so much as a glutton ogling a bounteous banquet table.

It was very late and the throng had thinned out considerably by the time Thomas saw an opening in the crowds around Caroline.

"You have scored a triumph," he told her. "Your name will be on the lips of all Mayfair before morning."

"Heaven forbid. If that is true, Aunt

Augusta will send me back to Sunnyslope tomorrow with Uncle Jeremy and Aunt Letitia."

"Not at all." He tucked her hand under his arm and led her toward the punch bowl. "If we simply stroll off, we can be alone enough to exchange reports. Not that I think you would have had time to gain any new intelligence this evening, but I do have a few items to report."

"I welcome all news. I suppose the gentlemen I find most attractive will be rascals."

"Lord Graham qualifies as a rascal most perfectly. Aunt Augusta's network has failed in his regard. The man is a rakehell at heart."

"Pity."

"Gaunt Gilbert was also enjoying Miss Langham's company."

"How sweet," she responded.

"After your one turn around the floor with him, Sir Reginald spent the rest of the evening in the card room. I fear you would be immensely bored with that gentleman."

"Perhaps. Did you dance with the Suitables? Any luck there?"

"I danced with all three. Miss Tyler's mother was in alt at being here 'at such a distinguished abode,' to quote her. Maria herself is not a bad sort, but is not smart enough to realize her money is the attraction, not her looks and certainly not her breeding. Miss Langham is perpetually tongue-tied, and Miss Oliver is quite the opposite. Spending time with her gives new meaning to the term 'verbose.' "

Caroline laughed. "It sounds so amusing until I consider the stakes involved. You have to settle on someone, and I do, too."

They wandered into the now empty card room. Only a few candles remained lit, and shadows danced on the walls and ceiling.

"I do not seem to have made much of an impression on the Suitables." Thomas stared down at a scattering of cards.

"Perhaps you're doing something wrong."

"Wrong?"

She touched his arm. "I mean, perhaps you are not flattering them enough. You know the routine. Give compliments."

"Such as, Miss Thornsnaggle, your squint seems to be improving?"

"I did not say you had to be truthful."

Thomas groaned. "Now the lady wants me to become a liar!"

"No, no. Use your imagination. Something metaphorical. Ruby lips, teeth like precious pearls, sparkling sapphire eyes."

"Miss Foulweather, your complexion is as green as emeralds."

Caroline wrinkled her nose and shook her head. "Use garden images. Complexion like a rose, eyes as blue as cornflowers, hair the shade of sundappled daisies."

"Whatever color that would be! Of course, you're correct as always, my dear Miss Parker. My skills as a lover are sadly inferior. I need instruction. What would a young man say to you right now to put you in a romantic mood?"

Caroline gazed at him. Words were hardly necessary to put her in a romantic mood when she stood beside him in the shadows. Life was so unfair, she thought, giving a big sigh.

Captain Ogden gave her a quizzical look. "Is it that impossible to visualize me as a potential lover?"

She shrugged, not wanting him to know the opposite was true. "First of all, you should stand very close and perhaps take her hand."

When he followed her directions, Caroline almost collapsed into his arms. Very gently he stroked her palm with his thumb.

Chills ran up her spine and she forced herself to go on. "Now remark on the beauty of the evening, how lovely she looks."

"Caroline, you are stunning in that gown. The light glimmers in your hair as if little stars were shining there."

Caroline felt her heart beating so rapidly she feared he would hear its thumping. Despite her best intentions, she leaned closer to him and when he lifted her hand to his lips, her knees went weak. Only with the greatest effort did she remind herself of their purpose.

Her voice was a whisper. "Perfect, Thomas. One more compliment or two, and then the kiss to seal the moment." She tried to pull away, but somehow his other arm had encircled her waist, trapping her. She looked up at him and tried to find words to break the spell, but she was speechless.

Slowly his lips neared hers, and the thundering of her heartbeat muted everything in her mind. Softly his mouth brushed hers. Then, like a shower of sparks, their lips met again, this time with passion. Deep within, a liquid fire dissolved her every hesitation, every uncertainty, every misgiving. The yearning ache in her heart consumed her, and she ran her fingers through his hair, secure in his embrace, willing the moment to last forever.

Approaching footsteps drove them apart. Wordlessly he steered her into the ball-room, where two servants began to straighten the chairs. For a long time nei-ther Thomas nor Caroline spoke. Then both began at once.

"Sorry, I got . . ." he said.

"I doubt you could . . ." she started.

Their eyes met and their tiny, tentative smiles grew to laughter.

"Which is worse?" he asked. "Being the teacher or the pupil? Both roles seem to get me into trouble."

"Your lessons are entirely too . . . too in-viting, I fear. Kissing is prohibited because it is too agreeable." With relief, Caroline felt her heartbeat returning to normal and her flush lessening.

Thomas took her arm again, and they strolled back to the Rose Saloon, where the remaining guests lingered over glasses of wine.

"Thomas! There you are!" Lady Eliza-beth looked relieved. "I was afraid you had forgotten me and gone on alone."

"Not likely. Miss Parker and I were simply checking to see if anyone was left under the card tables. I am pleased to re-port we found nary a laggard."

Thomas turned to Caroline, bowed, and touched his lips to her hand. "Miss Parker, all London worships you."

"Captain Ogden, all London questions your sincerity."

Once they had said good-bye to the last guest, Aunt Augusta led the family into her sitting room for a post-party discussion. Lord Barstow called for a bottle of brandy and declared the evening an unqualified success. Lady Clarissa sat beside Caroline and put her arm around her shoulder.

All eyes turned to Lady Augusta.

Her usually stern visage turned up a slight smile. "I think you did exceedingly well, my dear," she said.

Isabel, Letitia, and Ned began to talk at once, and Caroline put her head on her mother's shoulder. If only she could be as enthused as the rest of her family. If only she agreed with the intent of the whole charade. She had done as they all wished, bowed before the Queen, entertained the *ton,* and acquired her entrée to Almack's. For what purpose, she wondered.

She liked the wrong sort of man, the one with a raffish, albeit undeserved, reputation. Compared to Thomas Ogden, the others were dull, fastidious, ramshackle, or pompous conceited bores.

What was she to do? No alternative employment opportunities were evident. She saw women in London who had positions that might bring a degree of independence, but they all depended upon either a level of skill she did not possess or on a lack of virtue, virtue she had in spades. She was just as unqualified to become a governess as she was to set herself up as a courtesan, if the truth be known. Even the latter occupation was preferable to being the paid companion to some crochety, demanding old lady.

While the rest of the family celebrated, Caroline sat in silence, confused and tormented by self-pity.

Eleven

"Oh, I say, that is droll, don't you know?" The Countess of Napperton rolled her eyes and clapped her plump little hands in a mediocre imitation of a small child. "Just the sweetest wittle dears."

Caroline stopped the ponies beside Lady Napperton's pink-and-green cabriolet, struggling to ignore the elbow a giggling Isabel jabbed into her side.

"Good afternoon, my lady." Caroline offered a sugary smile. She recognized the baby face and tight little curls under a comically high-crowned pink satin bonnet. Aunt Augusta was eager for the opportunity to give the countess a cut direct, if Caroline had correctly overheard yesterday's maliciously toned teatime discourse.

Adorned in elaborate pink ruffles and feathers, the countess seemed hardly worthy of such censure. She waved her frilly pink parasol in their direction. "My dear, you must be Miss Parker. I have heard so much about your precious team of ponies and at last I see them myself."

Caroline dared a glance at Isabel. Aunt Augusta would most definitely not approve of their encounter with this person of dubious reputation, rumored to be among the Prince of Wales's closest friends.

"I am pleased you admire my team."

"Oh, Miss Parker, those dear beasts are just the thing, exactly suited to me. Their saucy little knees almost bump their pretty noses. I do adore them."

Caroline quashed a groan at the countess's description of the ponies' action. As if echoing Caroline's thoughts, Oberon snorted loudly and Puck pawed at the path.

The countess was attended by a lady in a sober dark green carriage dress and two footmen, as well as her driver. Caroline tried to guess Lady Napperton's age, with little success. She was certainly well beyond the first bloom.

"I do wish the dear Prince could see you," Lady Napperton continued. "Your most charming rig is *très chic*."

Caroline nodded. "Thank you."

"Adieu, adieu," the countess called as her carriage moved off.

Isabel and Caro exchanged glances again, and Caroline began to laugh. "Have you ever seen such an outfit? She seems to be masquerading as a pink-iced teacake — a whole platter of them as a matter of fact."

Ahead she could see two more carriages filled with stylish passengers. She had promised to be home well before the parade of the fashionables began, but here they were.

"Aunt Augusta will be in quite a pucker already. But it would hardly do to pass up a look at the procession, would it?"

"*Naturellement!*" Isabel waved her arm with a broad flourish.

Caroline sat up a bit straighter and headed the team into the thick of the *ton*'s daily afternoon jaunt to see and be seen. In minutes, several gentlemen on horseback hailed them, bowing in their saddles and tipping their hats in salute.

Caroline and Isabel waved and smiled, looking ahead to the oncoming clusters of carriages.

"An amazing variety," Caroline observed.

Isabel was wide-eyed at the sight of two brightly painted ladies riding by, their towering scarlet plumes waving in the breeze. "Ooh la, who are they?"

Caroline gasped. "Do not look. They are the fashionable impure, I believe. Forget

Aunt Augusta. If Mama hears about this, we are in big trouble."

As the traffic thickened, Caroline focused on keeping the ponies calm and collected, an easier task these days. If she did not know better, Caroline would have suspected the four animals deliberately had acquired the strutting swagger of London's parading dandies. With their high-stepping prance, the ponies' elegant bearing compared favorably to the finest bloodstock in the park.

"Oh, Caro, there's Captain Ogden."

Caroline felt her heartbeat race. "Driving Ned's pair. With Miss Tyler. Too bad she is not prettier." She pasted a sweet smile on her face and waved.

A loud voice boomed into her consciousness. "Fine cattle, miss!"

Caroline turned to a florid man on horseback, nodding her thanks, though she did not recognize him.

Thomas had passed by when she looked back. Was Maria pressed up tightly against him, she wondered. Certainly he could have found a larger equipage.

"Good afternoon, ladies. Lovely day." Lord Graham spoke from the high perch of a large barouche containing his mother, Lady Poynton, and an elderly, sharp-faced matron whose patrician air suggested a title of eminence.

Caroline slowed the ponies nearly to a stop.

"May I present Miss Parker and Lady Isabel Mortimer, your grace?" Lord Graham addressed the imposing lady. "The Duchess of Talbrook," he added to Caroline and Isabel.

"Honored, your grace, my lady," Caroline responded as the two ladies smiled. She saw Lady Poynton whispering animatedly into the duchess's ear as they passed by.

"At last an encounter Aunt Augusta will applaud."

"Actually, I thought the lightskirts were more interesting." Isabel renewed her elbowing.

Caroline signaled the team to pick up the pace a bit. Carriage after rider after curricle, smile after nod after wave of greeting, Caroline drove slowly, watching the ponies and the passing scene, yet strangely abstracted.

Maria Tyler was not the correct match for Thomas, she thought. The look on Maria's face a few minutes ago was far too smug. The girl must have a tediously vain streak, not at all the thing for a proper wife for him. Maria ought to be eliminated from the list of Suitables, and would be, just as soon as Caroline could talk with Thomas.

Thomas followed Charles Graham down the steps of Stafford House. "What's your pleasure, Charlie?"

"Might be a cat's paw or two ready to part with a few quid at Watier's," Graham replied. "Good for a few hours, anyway."

Thomas frowned to himself. He did not want to go back to the tables, but he saw no alternative. After the first expenses for the marquess and Josh, he had spent almost all his ready at his tailor. Lady Elizabeth insisted he be perfectly turned out, and he had to admit he had indulged his pride by refusing to allow his mother to pay a farthing toward his furnishings. Now with the need for more money in Somersetshire and at Aldon House, the demand for blunt became imperative.

"Only a few games for me." Thomas sighed, reluctant but resigned to his old pastime. Only a fool would rely on cards or dice as a way of life. London was full of fools, of course, of various size and purse, one more unpredictable than the next.

"Come now, Tom," Graham chided.

"Lost your taste for blood? Been as tame as a dove since your mama came to town."

Thomas refused to take the bait. For a number of years, his best asset had been his cool head. Tonight, when he had barely enough wherewithal for a stake at the Macao table, was a time to protect any advantage he could summon. No sense angering himself over Graham's rubbish.

When, a short time after midnight, they entered the card room, Thomas and Charles joined a group of young men who had barely begun the night's gaming.

"By Jove, Ogden," drawled Lord Rutledge, a consistently optimistic player. "It's about time you showed up. I'll have my revenge this evening!"

"Long memory, Rutledge." Thomas was not really surprised his defeats of the young lord were not forgotten. However, since Thomas sat with his first glass of claret of the evening and several of the players seemed well into their second or third bottle, he felt that no matter how the urge for revenge fired others, he had a great advantage over all of them. Before his prime opportunities would begin, he had several hours of play to endure.

The tedious conversation moved from

the various antics of the prince and his closest circle through the affairs of the absent Brummell to the mildly favorable news from the army. And eventually, the prospects and promise of this year's entrants into the marriage mart.

Lord Graham's speech was only slightly blurred as he swirled his claret. "The charms of Miss Caroline Parker outshine all the others combined."

Rutledge snickered. "Got some competition there, old man. Hear Longbury's hankering after her harness." The attempt at wit was met with spirited guffaws.

"Longbury is an ass," Graham declared, sneering.

Undaunted, Rutledge ploughed on. "Set after that chit and get a bit in your mouth just like 'er nags."

Thomas wanted to bury his fist in both their faces. Caroline was much too agreeable to be the subject of this drunken jawing. These clods were not worthy to mention her name. That Caroline had not immediately taken his suggestion to discourage Graham was more irritating than Thomas wanted to admit, and now his anger built dangerously high.

"Hear Baker has taken on a new bit 'o muslin." Thomas changed the subject immediately. "Quite a high flyer for such a priggish fellow."

"Count on it. She'll break his purse," Graham offered.

"One expensive canary." Lord Rutledge almost choked with ribald laughter, as the men assessed the fascinating attractions of females more attuned to appreciate the honor.

Thomas forced himself to wager conservatively, once in a while purposely giving up a winning hand to Rutledge. The room was noisy with the rumble of taut voices, harsh laughter and the occasional loud curse. Thomas had not remembered the oppressive heat or the annoying distractions, the sour taste of his few sips of wine. To protect his meager stake, his bets were often smaller than usual.

"Where's your mettle, Ogden?" one player complained when Thomas refused to boost on a chancy card.

"Deplorable pigeon-heartedness," sneered Rutledge. "Ain't got daring in mind?"

Thomas ignored the taunts, though his tension grew as his take increased by the smallest of increments. Just wait, he cautioned himself. Graham had nothing to lose but more worthless vowels, but Rutledge and several others were quite plump in the pocket, too ripe for the picking to abandon over specious twaddle.

In another hour, Thomas's jaw ached from clamping back the invective he wished to pour over his tablemates, and his head throbbed from the effort of remaining still. All the players were about even in winnings, none having done great damage to any other. For the next three hands, Thomas carefully watched the other players. None of them was in his cups, but all certainly were on the verge.

Little by little Thomas increased the bets, and Rutledge responded in kind, slowly drifting into the realm of reckless betting. Thomas matched the size of the bets, each hand endangering the entire night's spoils, but he concealed his anxiety in feigned fearlessness. He called to the waiter. "Bring another bottle. I need another draught of valor."

Rutledge laughed, if a bit uneasily. "That's like my ol' mate. Now we'll have some sport."

Wagers on the next hands were perilously high. Three losing hands in a row and Thomas knew he would be finished. He would not, could not, write out any worse-than-useless vowels.

His eventual success depended upon his

ability to outmatch the others. Two of the players looked about ready to drop out or pass out where they sat. Hours of drinking had dulled their skills, but Thomas hoped his senses were still sharp. The time had come to make his move, doubling the bets, winning three, then losing two. The others fell into the doubling habit, and carefully Thomas bided his time. Hundreds of pounds rode on each deal.

Now if the cards were fair, if he had just a tiny edge of luck, if none of the others were dissembling . . . Graham wrote the first of his notes. Two players dropped out. Thomas allowed himself a sly smile as Graham and the others folded, leaving him alone with Rutledge. Between them, all the evening's wagers lay on the table.

"By Hector, I'll have you this time," Rutledge muttered to Thomas, as he dealt the cards. "All or nothing."

Thomas nodded, shrugging. He peeked at his cards. Godawful fate, the worst combination, the longest odds. He kept his face impassive, but his only hope was that Rutledge would take too many cards and shatter the limit. Thomas shook his head, refusing another card and standing on his present holding, however impossible. The next card was bound to break him.

The pause seemed endless. The candles burned low and he looked around to see the room was almost empty. Rutledge stared at his cards, swaying a bit from side to side. Thomas waited as, one by one, his futile hopes for the night's winnings seemed to float away in the close air. Fickle, fickle luck . . . a fool's bedmate. At last, Rutledge flipped over one more card, a six. Thomas felt a cold jolt in his gut. He should have taken it himself. Now his fate was sealed.

Then to Thomas's amazement, Rutledge began to laugh, a bitter cackle that chilled the very air of the room. "At least you did not get my horse tonight!" He threw his cards on the table and stalked out.

For a few moments, Thomas did not move. He felt the sweat trickle down his spine. Amazingly he had won, though he took no pride in the result. The pile of money sitting before him would be well spent, but this was the end. The last time. He felt thoroughly filthy.

Following Sunday's services, Caroline accompanied her mother into a circle of ladies surrounding Mrs. Oliver and her daughter, Georgina. The pale blue sky was streaked with wispy clouds, and a mild breeze fluttered the skirts of the ladies gathered outside the church. The morning air felt damply fresh after the night's heavy rains.

"Such a lovely party," a portly matron in lilac effused.

Others immediately took up the praise, acclamations on the previous evening's ball for Georgina. Exaggerated compliments, Caroline thought. The gathering had been no different than a dozen others she had attended.

Sighing, she wandered away from the chattering group. A flower vendor peddled her wares from an enormous basket of blooms, another girl eking out a living in London. Where did she live, Caroline wondered. Did the flower girl earn any more than the women who tinted the printed fashion plates, one by one, with watercolors?

Caroline had thought Georgina's ball quite dull, without even the dubiously diverting attention of her usual suitors. Neither Lord Graham, whose gossipy remarks were sometimes entertaining, nor Lord Longbury, whose comic if silent antics caused an occasional smile, had graced the party. After a single turn about the floor with her, Sir Reginald had retired, as usual, to the card room. Most of her dances were with Ned or his friends, none of them held in high regard by Aunt Augusta. Captain Ogden discharged himself well, dancing attention on the honored Miss Oliver. In fact, he had overdone himself quite disgracefully. He had practically fawned over the chit.

Now as she gazed across the pavement, she tried to see Georgina through Thomas's eyes. Her ruched satin bonnet was outlandishly overdone, as was the matching cape, both in a shade of tangerine too vivid for Caroline's taste. Caroline tried to shake off her disapproval. Her feelings were precisely contrary to the goodwill and charity encouraged by this morning's services.

As she watched, Thomas Ogden brought Georgina a spray of lilies of the valley, causing a cascade of exclamations Caroline heard from a considerable distance. Georgina had an unpleasantly shrill voice, even at this distance, and the way she slipped her hand under Thomas's arm seemed purposely possessive. Then Thomas presented Mrs. Oliver with an identical corsage. Mrs. Oliver appeared to be quite overcome, and Thomas's gallant gesture caused no end of approbation among the gathered ladies.

Thomas himself looked as handsome as ever, Caroline thought. But after his shamelessly ingratiating gesture, he seemed to lean heavily on his walking stick. Between last night's dancing and the dampness, he must be in some pain. He should have stayed in bed this morning.

Eager to avert her eyes from the scene, Caroline whirled around and abruptly stepped into a large puddle. The muddy water soaked her slipper and splattered over the hem of her white skirt. "Damnation," she muttered, feeling the wetness seep through her stocking to her toes.

"Caroline!" Her cousin Ned's voice was urgent, as he hurried toward her. "You will never believe . . ."

"Look at this!" she urged, pointing at her dripping shoe. For once Caroline was grateful to see her cousin. "They should have had the water swept up . . ."

Ned paid no attention. "I met the Countess of Napperton last night."

"Where in the world were you?"

"No matter. When she heard I am your kin, she spoke of nothing but the ponies. She wants to buy them for herself."

"What? They are not for sale. Especially not to the likes of her."

"Why not? She thinks you are a rare spirited chit, to quote her exactly. At least find out how much she'll give you for the nags."

Her sopping foot momentarily forgotten, Caroline saw the group around Georgina beginning to part. Just as she suspected, Thomas Ogden stuck to the Oliver ladies like a leech. "Aunt Augusta says Lady Napperton is a social-climbing mushroom."

"Aw, Aunt Grumbletonian don't have the last word on everyone, you know."

"Well, I admit I am a bit curious about how much she would offer."

"Caroline, your shoe is all wet!"

"Indeed!" she snapped. "And it is cold."

"Good morning, Ned." Lady Clarissa joined them. "I did not realize you were at services."

"Er, I was not, Aunt Clarissa. I came looking for, ah, Caroline."

"No matter. Now perhaps you would like to escort us home." Clarissa began to take his arm.

"I'd be honored if you'd but join Miss Langham and her mother. I, ah, am pledged to walk their way . . ."

Clarissa's smile was as broad as Caroline's was surprised. "You go on. Caroline and I will make our own way."

As she and her mother began to walk toward Barstow House, Caroline felt the water squish out of her shoe. Her head felt quite addled with the morning's surprise events. Cousin Ned competing with Thomas for Louisa Langham? Lady Napperton actually offering to buy the ponies? And Thomas pinning posies on Georgina *and* her mother? Events were beginning to spin out of all control.

And she had ruined a perfectly good kid slipper.

Twelve

Caroline watched Louisa Langham nervously twist her handkerchief as they waited to sing. Why should she be jittery? Judging from the young lady now playing, she needed only to stay in the neighborhood of the melody to comport herself adequately. Caroline diverted her eyes from Miss Langham before her obvious trepidation rubbed off.

Although the setting in Lady Kimball's ballroom was elegant and the audience of leading members of the *ton* were perfectly turned out in their silks and laces, diamonds and pearls, none of those within Caroline's view seemed to be paying much attention to the proceedings. To them, these short and merely competent, if not outright awkward, performances were simply a justification for the gathering. A little musical version of the real purpose of the evening: to see and be seen while exchanging the latest Society rumors of scandal and outrage.

Caroline smiled to herself. The luxuriousness of the surroundings and the resplendence of the fashions now seemed almost stale. One elegant town house appeared awfully like another, perhaps because they were so often stuffed to bursting with ladies and gentlemen milling about like sheep in a tightly packed pen. At the moment, the barking animal holding them all at bay in their places was a young lady wailing about a lonesome cuckoo bird to the plunking accompaniment of her mother at the pianoforte.

Caroline gazed at the brilliant chandelier above her head. Thousands of crystal drops reflected tiny rainbows from a hundred candles. If she squinted her eyes, the transformed image seemed a myriad of iridescent halos glittering above, sparkling and shimmering as she swayed.

"Caroline," her mother whispered. "Do not squirm so."

Caroline sighed and looked down at her gauzy white skirt. She wore a simple gown with a blue satin sash and matching ribbons woven through her hair. The outfit reminded her of a christening gown for an infant.

Beside her Louisa continued to mangle her handkerchief, her face pale and anxious. When the polite applause signaled her turn, Caroline walked to the front of the room. She was surprised to see a row of young gentlemen lounging against the back wall, Cousin Ned, Simon Ogden, Lord Longbury, and Captain Ogden among them. She hoped Louisa would be too preoccupied and fearful to notice.

When she took her place at the piano-forte, Caroline recalled her aunt's instructions. She turned and smiled at the audience before striking the opening chords. Just as Aunt Augusta had predicted, Caro's frequent repetitions at practice indeed made the words and tune flow easily, effortlessly. When she completed her first ballad, Caroline was surprised to hear rather enthusiastic applause, much of it coming, she noted, from the very rear of the room. She gave the audience a genuine smile this time and launched into her second presentation, a little sonatina she did not need to sing. Even so, she felt a great sense of relief steal over her as she completed the final arpeggio. To generous clapping, she made her curtsy and took her seat. Caroline glanced at Lady Augusta, who was almost smiling, a near huzzah from her aunt.

"Very fine, my dear," Lady Clarissa whispered.

Caroline nodded to her mother and squeezed Louisa's hand as she rose shakily to perform.

Louisa's frightened expression was directed only at the keyboard, Caroline noted, which was just as well, considering the poor girl's tension. Luck was with Louisa, however, for she completed her song without a flaw. Again Caroline could tell the most enthusiastic applause came from the rear of the room.

After two more young ladies submitted themselves to the torment of trying to entertain the inattentive gathering, the musicale ended. As the audience dispersed to fresh pursuits, Caroline and Louisa found themselves surrounded with the congratulations of their friends and family.

Amidst the accolades, Caroline watched for Thomas, who offered his congratulations to Louisa. As the others moved toward the refreshments, Caroline caught his eye and lagged behind. They strolled back to the pianoforte and stood under the chandelier.

"Perhaps you have found a new professional opportunity? I warn you, however, the opera stage would hardly please your aunt. In fact, she might succumb to a permanent sort of swoon."

"Not a completely displeasing prospect."

Thomas looked his impeccable best, with an elaborate cravat and ivory waistcoat in stark contrast to the severe black coat which hugged his broad shoulders. The faintest trace of his spicy orange scent tickled her senses. What would he do if she reached up and played with the curls on his forehead or caressed his cheek?

Thomas appeared to be oblivious of her admiration. "My report is rather brief so far. Apparently Lord Graham and Sir Reginald are not fond of such entertainments as tonight's."

He paused, devilishly lifting one eyebrow. "However, Lord Longbury was totally enthralled and captivated. I believe his hands will be useless for the rest of the evening, so severe must be their sting from the fervor of his applause. If his tongue had hung out half an inch more, I would have declared him a wolf at the henhouse door."

"Or perhaps the village idiot." Caroline's fingertips tingled as though she had really touched his cheek or run her fingers through his hair.

"What? Are you belittling that most faithful of your Eligibles?"

"No, not really." Thomas acted distant

this evening, Caroline thought. Not even the tiniest of insinuations or the most casual of touches sparked their exchange.

"We have left Lord Longbury with Miss Langham, you know. With the defection this evening of your formerly faithful Lord Graham and the consistent indifference of Sir Reginald . . ."

"What do you mean, indifference? He's not one of you young nodcocks, spending most of his time chasing skirts. He is more like . . . like Aunt Augusta's husband, Sir Barnaby. He has the respect of many . . ."

"And who was the young lady who said having Sir Barnaby around was like being accompanied by a particularly thoughtful and silent footman? Is that what you want in a husband?"

"Don't twist my words!" Caroline knew she sounded snappish.

"Then attend to mine! Lord Longbury is winning by default if tonight is any measure of the race. Perhaps we should attempt to add to your list of Eligibles, Caroline."

"Name a few candidates!"

"I will look around." He paused, then spoke softly, only half aloud. "Certainly no one from the group at Watier's."

"At Watier's? You were there? When?"

"Ah, Caro, I know I should not have, but I needed . . ."

"You are positively addled, Thomas Ogden!"

"Now, now. I did not mean to break any of your rules. Or Aunt Augusta's or my mother's, either."

"Whosc rules indeed? You were the one who made those rules. Remember? You said that none of the young ladies you court would be allowed even to dance with a card shark. And now, you, you feather-brain!"

"Really, I had to . . . I, that is I wanted to buy sheep for Josh, and . . ."

"Here I am grinding my fingers to nubs on the keys and straining my voice, playing and singing. And all the while you are fresh from a den of vice, ruining your reputation and any chance you might have of winning consent from the moneybags Langham's father. You are a complete waste of my time and effort!"

Thomas's voice was heavy with irony. "Come now, my dove. Your delicate little pinkies are none the worse for your performance, which, I might add, showed you to full advantage before a roomful of the *ton*'s high and mighty. Perhaps you have your cap set on some elderly gentleman whose foot is already poised at the edge of his hereafter. There were several of that ilk present tonight."

"Yes, such a doddering fellow is exactly what I need! And I should have thought you might have identified someone like that by now, before you are turned out of Mayfair's ballrooms for gambling."

"If a bit of gambling was a cause for exclusion, every ballroom in London would be empty!" His glare softened. "Miss Twistnozzle, your cheeks are as scarlet as Prinny's waistcoat and your eyes are as luminous as a jellied eel."

Caroline gasped, then began to giggle in spite of her anger.

"Please continue my lessons in courtship, Miss Parker. I fear I am lamentably in need of further instruction."

"Humpf!" Caroline snorted through her laughter. "After your presentation of flowers to Miss Oliver's mother last Sunday, I am inclined to declare you a certified dandy."

"Surely not. Truce, Miss Parker?" His voice, barely a murmur, sent chills up her spine.

"Truce." She moistened her lips and returned his gaze, hardly moving.

He reached for her hand and silently led

her through a door, away from the noisy, well-lit room. The back corridor was shadowy. With no further hesitation, he pulled her into his arms.

"You see, I remain highly improp—"

Caroline cut off his words with her mouth on his. Of her own accord, she pressed her body against his, and he wrapped his arms tightly around her.

His spicy fragrance and warm embrace crumbled the wall she had tried to build against her growing emotional vulnerability to him. How could she consider spending her life with anyone but Thomas? She kissed him with all the sweet passion in her soul.

When at last they broke apart, she felt tears in her eyes. "How could this happen?"

He cradled her in his arms and sighed. "How? I am hardly the person to ask, Caro. I feel helpless myself. I know we are endangering all we seek, yet I cannot help myself."

"Nor can I." He sought her lips again and she melted into his long, tender kiss.

A footman with a tray of glasses pointedly cleared his throat from down the hall.

She pulled away, and stood still for a

moment to quiet her pounding heart, her breathless gasps.

Thomas tucked her hand under his arm and moved aside to let the footman pass, then led her back into the ballroom. No one had noticed their absence nor observed their return. Only her still-rapid heartbeat betrayed the brief interlude. She smiled at him, almost afraid to find a look of shame. "By the way, how much did you win?"

Thomas grinned. "You wound me, madam."

"Never say you lost!"

"Josh will have his flock and funds to repair a house for his family, but that is all. The cards are too fickle."

"Oh, so you are indeed reformed? Can I assure Miss Oliver's papa of this, or will you next be at the gaming table for a gaggle of geese?"

Caroline beamed with pride as she drove the ponies down Piccadilly to pull up before Hatchards.

"Just think, Isabel, the team behaves quite tolerably and this is one of the busiest streets in London."

"*Oui, très bon.*"

Aunt Augusta was sleeping extra late that morning, a result, Ellis informed them, of a headache for which she had dosed her mistress with a strong powder. Rather a few too many sherries last evening, Caroline suspected.

Isabel was anxious to buy a horrific novel recommended by none other than Miss Oliver, who had called yesterday. Miss Oliver, while missish in the extreme, cultivated Caroline's friendship. Isabel theorized that Miss Oliver heard of the attention the pony drives received and wished to be invited along.

Near the bookstore, almost before the tiger took the bridles of the ponies, Sir Reginald Sedgewick reached up to assist Caroline's descent.

"Why, good morning, Miss Parker. What a fortunate coincidence to meet you this fine day."

Inwardly Caroline groaned. The last thing she needed was to meet Reg the Veg, as she and Thomas had christened him in honor of his lack of consequence, which they likened to a spot of mashed eggplant or overcooked green peas.

"Good day, Sir Reginald. Perhaps you would be so kind as to attend to my mother," she suggested waving to the carriage stopping behind them.

He helped her down, then turned to Lady

Clarissa. Isabel rolled her eyes and Caroline grimaced at his back. They actually were pleasantly surprised when both Lady Clarissa and Sir Reginald stopped immediately inside the entrance to greet more acquaintances. Caroline and Isabel beckoned to Peg and headed for the rear of the store.

"This is the agricultural section," Isabel complained.

Caroline leaned close and whispered. "Anything is better than being forced to listen to that man prose on. He is so dull that . . ."

Thomas Ogden looked up from his scrutiny of a thick volume. "Why, ladies, how nice to see you." He closed the book and held it behind his back.

"What were you so engrossed in?" Caroline asked.

"Oh, nothing. Just browsing a bit." His grin looked a little guilty.

"I suspect Captain Ogden is scanning the latest novel from the Minerva Press." Caroline nudged Isabel.

"Please let me see," Isabel said. "Perhaps you have found one I have not read."

"Well, ah, this is not a novel," Thomas said. "You would not be in the least interested."

Caroline was fascinated at his evident

discomfiture. What about the book made him so flustered? "He seems to think we are frivolous gels, Isabel, worthy only of the most sensational prose."

Thomas shook his head in mock disgust. "You are a pest of the first water, Miss Parker." He handed her the heavy volume. "Simply a dull tome on estate management."

Caroline laughed. "Why, Captain Ogden, how diligent of you. I would have guessed it was a treatise on oriental harem administration."

"Ogden, ladies." Sir Reginald, his voice booming, joined them. "Ah, see you have the Portland book there, Ogden. Excellent work, that. That gray volume on animal husbandry is top-notch, too."

When she later thought back on the morning, Caroline could not quite sort out how it happened that Thomas and Sir Reginald had gone off to luncheon at their club with armloads of books, while she and the ladies had been content with a single purchase and the company of no gentlemen at all. But she certainly admired Captain Ogden's zeal for learning how to make Aldonhurst flourish.

Under near cloudless skies, Caroline and

260

her mother rode in the pony phaeton toward Richmond Park. Isabel, Aunt Augusta, Ned, and Simon followed in the brougham. The country jaunt offered a perfect test for the ponies over a longer distance in traffic. In their four-in-hand harness, the latter pair, Puck and Ariel, did fine as the wheelers, carrying most of the weight of the miniature phaeton. The forward pair, Oberon and Titania, set the pace as the flashier of the duos.

Traffic thinned as they left Mayfair behind, though the road remained busy. Like themselves, many were out enjoying the mild weather and the glories of flower-strewn fields.

If it had not had a darker import for her, Caroline would have welcomed the summer. But this year, the warm weather had ominous implications. What would happen to her as the Season drew to a close? She had failed utterly to find a reasonable occupation for independence. And she had failed to sway her mother from the determination to have her wed by autumn.

Lady Clarissa shaded her face with a striped silk parasol. "Caroline, my dear, we have hardly managed a moment alone in the past few weeks."

"I never would have imagined so many

parties, Mama. So many people, so many dresses."

"And, tell me true, have you enjoyed the festivities? Perhaps just a little bit?"

"Mama, I own I have been having a wonderful time. But there is a shadow hanging over every rout, every musicale. My enjoyment is lessened by the concern that somewhere in the crowd lurks my future husband, looking at me, measuring me against who knows what standard."

"Silly goose. Why are you concerned? Every eligible man in town seems to have sent you flowers. Why, the house smells like a bower of lilies, and the buds hardly have time to blossom fully before more bouquets arrive."

"I am sure many girls find their sitting rooms crowded with posies."

"I am not certain of that at all. You are an unqualified success, beyond even my most optimistic expectations. Your Aunt Augusta is delighted."

"And probably quite astonished."

"Caroline, sometimes I think you have a sassy streak."

Caroline laughed out loud. "Mama, darling, surely you have noticed my unfortunate tongue before."

The phaeton covered the distance

quickly, Caroline thinking about the team or fretting at her few options, Clarissa exclaiming at the new construction and the road improvements they encountered. Caroline had sent a note to Thomas suggesting he bring Miss Langham and her mother to the picnic. They were to pretend it was a coincidence, but as the team entered the park, Caroline saw the lovely May day had inspired many similar excursions. Several groups had spread their nuncheons on cloths or tables provided by liveried servants. It took only a few moments to locate and join the Ogden party.

Will, the groom, took the reins of the phaeton from Caroline and unharnessed the ponies, hobbling them for their first quiet grazing opportunity since the animals had arrived in town. Like her ponies, Caroline gave herself up to the indolence of the day, listening to the others talk and laugh.

She watched Thomas entertain Miss Langham with unexpressed envy. How had life become so difficult? Caroline had never thought herself capable of real jealousy, but here it was, intruding on her every moment. She felt a wave of nostalgia for the uncomplicated days at Sunnyslope when she and Isabel often carried a basket to a little glen or a grassy spot beside the river. How long ago it seemed.

Aunt Augusta had thoughtfully provided a decanter of sherry, and after a generous glass and an equally generous repast, that lady actually allowed herself to lounge against a tree and drift off. Caroline looked about her. Miss Langham and Isabel talked with Ned and Lord Longbury. Caroline watched them carefully. Perhaps this was a good time to question Thomas about the next stage of their plans.

"Walk with me by the pond," she suggested.

Caroline and Thomas strolled through the grass. He offered his arm as they neared the edge of the pond. He was as handsome as any man she had encountered in London, and the sound of his deep voice was pleasing to the ear, more so in comparison to the whinish drone of Lord Longbury.

This was no time to slip into forbidden dreams, she reminded herself. "I wish you could have seen the ponies. They were most elegant and refined. Nothing in the traffic seemed to bother them."

"You must be pleased and proud. They have passed every trial you could devise. Are you considering the offer from Lady

Napperton? You could invest the money in additional stock."

"I could, if I were to stay at Sunnyslope. But how long can I impose upon my uncle and his family?" Caroline took off her chip straw bonnet and shook out her curls, running her fingers through the tangles.

"Your aunt will need her vinaigrette if she sees you without that flower garden on your head."

She looked at the hat ruefully. "Out here in the middle of nature, these phony flowers look ridiculous. Look at the wild roses, how much more beautiful they are than these silly things."

"I would never contradict that notion." He broke off a small branch adorned with clusters of pink and exuding the fragrance most beloved in the kingdom.

"I think the silk flowers are like all of London Society, the clothes, the manners, the music, the food. All of them are aberrations of nature, perversions of reality. Do you agree?"

He nodded. "Of course, the parallel is appropriate, but I think it is done for a reason. Everything in Society moves more quickly, as though distilled from the natural process, keeping only the essences and extracting them as a method of speeding up nature. And with one outcome in mind: furtherance of the leading families through courtship, marriage, and procreation."

"You sound almost respectful. Do you approve of Society's ways now?"

Thomas laughed. "As a philosopher, I apparently leave something to be desired, Miss Parker. But to be honest, if I can overlook the necessity to court the Suitables, I have rather enjoyed this Season. And I suspect you have, too."

Now it was Caroline's turn to smile.

They sat in the long grass beside the pond, sheltered from the sunshine by an ancient oak. Daisies and buttercups were scattered alongside them. The old roses on the branch she held in her hand perfumed the air. Silence reigned apart from the singing of insects and, from time to time, distant laughter.

Thomas wore an open-collared shirt with a dotted scarf knotted about his throat, and the breeze tousled his hair. He looked quite dashing, like a romantic pirate or a highwayman, and she would follow him anywhere if he but asked.

He would not ask, of that she was certain. She had no fortune, merely a skimpy dowry, nowhere near what he required for the restoration of Aldonhurst.

But what about his attentions to the muslin set? He never hid his intentions to find his pleasures away from his wife. She would never forget his dreadful words. At the moment, he was too busy pursuing a wife to have much time for dalliance, she surmised. He did not plan to love his wife, that he had already decided.

She lay back in the grass, listening to the buzz of bees as they went from flower to flower, absorbed in their task. From time to time a lark called, summoning an answer from afar. The rural peace of the setting made her yearn for Sunnyslope, and unaccountably she began to feel a lump in her throat and tears gathering.

Caroline wanted to cry for her childhood, now behind her forever, and for the thought of losing the ponies. And especially she wanted to weep because she would lose Thomas, and lose him to one of the Suitables, one of that impossible trio he would never love.

Or perhaps he would, she thought. Perhaps he would come to love the woman he married after all. But she would never love anyone else but Thomas. She would never fall in love with one of the Eligibles no matter how long she had to live with him.

Thirteen

In the drawing room, Monsieur Sable asked questions to which Isabel replied. Quite proficiently, Caroline thought, as she gazed on the flowers adorning every space in the room. There were so many of them she had lost count.

"Mademoiselle Parker, s'il vous plaît," Monsieur said. *"Réciter les couleurs des fleurs."*

"Je vois rouge, et bleu, et jaune, et blanc . . ."

"Très bien, Mlle. Parker. Répondre, s'il vous plaît, vous avez . . ."

Finally the tedious lessons were finished. Isabel escorted M. Sable to the door and wished him a fond adieu. More than anything except the dancing lessons, Isabel adored learning French phrases. Isabel's affectation of elegant refinements continually amused Caroline.

Aunt Augusta, followed by Lady Clarissa, came into the room, and sat down with an air of gravity.

"Sir Barnaby and I will be leaving you

for a few days, my dear. We think it would be wise to see to things at home. And with my daughter Sarah in a rather delicate condition, I do wish to see how she is coming along. Then, plans for my yearly garden party for the parish must begin. We will return within a fortnight, I am sure. In the meantime, Clarissa assures me that you and Isabel will not deviate from the strict protocols we have established."

Caroline could hardly believe her good fortune. A respite from Augusta's carping and a time alone with her mother — or nearly alone — was just what she wanted. "Oh, I assure you, we will do quite well here."

"I have reason to believe Lord Longbury and Sir Reginald are both poised to make an offer for you soon. As I suggested last month, I recommend you discourage Lord Graham. Not in a discourteous way of course, but I do believe his mama is equivocating about his overindulgence at the tables."

Augusta turned to her younger sister. "Clarissa, you must have the gentleman wait until Sir Barnaby can hear his suit. But I doubt that anyone worth having will be unaware of our absence. Try if you can to drop a few hints that we will be thinking over an offer quite soon. See if we can move them right along."

"Quite so," Lady Clarissa agreed.

Caroline was proud of her own restraint. Not until she and Isabel were safely preparing for bed did she pound her pillow and squeal in delight.

The next morning, after conveying several detailed lists to Caroline, Isabel, Clarissa, and the staff, the Stolpers departed in their carriage. Ellis and Sir Barnaby's man followed with the luggage in a second equipage.

Silently Caroline and Isabel embraced, careful that the servants would not overhear their glee.

Caroline kept her voice a whisper. "Can you imagine? She wants me to give out all sorts of misinformation and try to bam someone into coming up to scratch."

"If you use those words to her, she would surely chastise you for using vulgar cant." Isabel smothered a giggle.

Caroline turned to Lady Clarissa. "Mama, do you think we might have a visit to the Tower of London this afternoon? We have both been ever so eager to see it."

Clarissa shook her head. "You have Monsieur Sable and the music master. There will not be time afterward."

"Oh, please, just this once?"

Clarissa smiled, her blue eyes twinkling. "Tomorrow will be time enough. We will tell the gentlemen we are engaged tomorrow, and this afternoon we will have to be content with a visit to Gunter's instead."

"Oh, thank you, Mama."

The next day's visit to the Tower was as thrilling as the girls had expected, and they were truly fatigued by the time they arrived home. Clarissa, however, was met at the door by the butler, who looked most befuddled.

"You have a gentleman caller, Lady Clarissa. He has been waiting these past two hours, a Count Lagerstrom."

As soon as she heard the name, Clarissa flew up the stairs.

Caroline's bewildered shrug was returned by Isabel.

"Who is Count Lagerstrom?" Caroline did not expect an answer.

Both girls headed up the stairs. At the halfway point, Caroline heard her mother's voice, full of excitement.

"I am so glad you came. I want you to meet my daughter and my niece. My sister and her husband just left for a few days, but surely you will stay long enough to meet them."

Caroline stood at the entrance of the drawing room when her mother called. Caroline was more curious than ever now that she saw the tall and handsome blond man of middle years.

"My dear, I want you to meet my friend from Stockholm, Count Lagerstrom, who is here on a diplomatic mission. David, my daughter, Caroline, and my niece, Lady Isabel Mortimer."

He took Caroline's hand and bowed low over it. "I am charmed to make your acquaintance." He had only a hint of an accent. "Your mother speaks of you often, and I knew you would be quite as lovely as she is and as she had described you."

Caroline curtsied and smiled, though she did not quite know how to react to this debonair gentleman who seemed so special to her mother. Isabel received the same charming presentation.

"We have been on a little tour, David, to the Tower of London. Had I but known you would be arriving, we would have waited."

"I will be most delighted to escort you three lovely ladies anywhere. I may even know about some interesting spots in your capital that you are not aware of." He turned to the girls and explained. "I was part of the Swedish delegation to King George for a number of years and truly enjoyed my sojourn in England."

The next evening at Lady Reston's musicale, Caroline sang, followed by Louisa Langham. After the other girls finished performing, Caroline was amazed to see Thomas and Ned again in the audience.

Thomas gave her a polite bow. "Miss Parker, your performance was very fine."

She looked at him through narrowed eyes. "Are you gammoning me again?"

"No, indeed. I am sincere. You and Miss Langham do yourselves proud."

"Or, Captain Ogden, are you developing a tendre for Miss Langham? She is certainly the best of the current crop of Suitables, in my opinion." Caroline meant the words, however much they hurt. She kept her voice light, but she felt the sting of envy and tried to cover her chagrin with a brave smile.

Count Lagerstrom and Lady Clarissa came forward to congratulate her on a fine performance.

"May I present my cousin, Lord Edward Mortimer, and Captain Thomas Ogden?" Caroline addressed the count, who responded with enthusiasm.

The men immediately became involved

in a conversation about the progress of the war, the recent treaty between England and Sweden's Prince Bernadotte, and the probability that Napoléon could at last be brought to heel. Caroline enjoyed listening to them, but was soon drawn away by Lord Longbury.

Caroline knew he intended to propose again the visit to Westminster Abbey. Since she desired as large a group as could be formed, she hoped to include Miss Langham, Ned, Isabel, and the others.

Eventually the party was made up for the following day. Caroline smiled to herself. She had developed a real skill at this sort of maneuvering. The group would assemble at the east front at one. Lord Longbury was gratified to be asked to guide the group and say a few words about the abbey's architecture. Not that he would need any encouragement.

The next morning, after her drive with the ponies, Caroline went into the breakfast room and chose a slice of toast at the sideboard.

"Ring for hot coffee, please dear." Lady Clarissa sat at the table going through a stack of invitations to upcoming routs and entertainments.

Caroline could not contain her curiosity.

"Tell me about the count. He is ever so handsome."

Her mother looked up quickly. "Oh, yes. David, the count, is a very fine person." She returned her attention to the stack of cards.

"Mama, do you have a little romantic interest —"

"He is married. Of course I have no thought of . . . you see, his wife is ill, an invalid. That is, she is not in her right mind and never will be. She will forever need constant care."

"How very sad."

"I suppose it would be too naughty of us to defy Augusta's wishes and attend the Brevorts' masquerade," Clarissa said, half to herself.

"I think it sounds quite delicious." Caroline knew Lady Augusta would be horrified.

"What sounds delicious?" Isabel entered the room and took a place at the table. "Is there some new confectionery you are keeping secret from me?"

Both ladies laughed and assured Isabel that although she was not in on the evening's entertainment, she had a full range of London's delights at her hand, including that very afternoon a visit to the Abbey.

"But whatever is so delicious? Another church?"

Lady Clarissa sipped her coffee. "No, hardly, although it should be quite educational. I was referring to a card received to a masquerade, but I fear Augusta would think me quite lacking in sense if I allowed Caroline to attend."

As her mother opened the next envelope, Caroline and Isabel exchanged a speaking glance. Neither young lady dared voice her thoughts, but neither doubted the other's thinking. When Lady Clarissa turned to pour another cup, Caroline neatly slid the masquerade invitation onto her lap under her napkin.

One after another the cards were opened, discussed, and sorted into two piles, one for affirmative replies, the other for negatives. Caroline and Isabel toyed with their toast, waiting until they could be alone, but Lady Clarissa took no notice of their lack of attention. She chatted on about the afternoon's tour, solicited the girls' opinions on sportier feathers for the hat matching her riding costume, and admired the white orchid floating in a crystal bowl on the table, sent to her by Count Lagerstrom. Eventually, just as Caroline was about to give up on dawdling at the table for another boring moment, Lady Clarissa excused herself to go upstairs. Caroline looked around to be sure none of the servants was present. She pulled the card out and gleefully showed it to Isabel.

"Perhaps I should not, but I find this ever so tempting!"

Isabel was more than enthusiastic. "If we go in costume, I can go along, too. No one will know who I am."

"Would not Aunt Augusta fall into a faint! I do not know, Isabel, if we dare. But then why not? We can make our escape before the midnight unmasking. Can we keep it a secret from Mama?"

"If Peg agrees to help us. What can we wear as costumes?"

"Something simple, something we can assemble without raising anyone's suspicions."

"We can ask Thomas and Simon Ogden to escort us. Better not tell Ned. He never remembers when he is supposed to be discreet."

Caroline noted the particulars of the ball and carefully returned the invitation to the discard stack.

Caroline stabbed the needle into the straw of her bonnet, trying to anchor new trimming. She pulled the thread tight, then aimed for a second stitch, instead pricking nothing but the skin of her thumb.

"Ouch!" she moaned, quickly sticking the thumb into her mouth. The roses that once adorned the brim of her bonnet lay strewn on the carpet, frayed and torn. Afternoon sun poured through the windows, highlighting the limp petals and twisted stems as though they were part of dead and discarded bouquets. Good thing I have not decided to seek my fortune as a milliner, she thought.

Of course, because she tried to hurry, everything went wrong. Count Lagerstrom would be here any minute to call for her, Isabel, and Lady Clarissa. They were due at the Abbey in less than half an hour.

Determinedly she took up the needle again and carefully inserted the point, pushing it through with the edge of her scissors. "There! I've finished the difficult part."

"Part of what?" Isabel was fully primed to depart, hat in place and gloves in hand.

"I am changing the trim . . ." Caroline began.

Isabel interrupted. "Oh, the lovely flowers, Caroline. What happened to them?" She knelt and picked up two of the bedraggled roses.

"I tired of them. What do you think of this?" Caroline held up a mass of blue and white bows with long trailing streamers. "If you will help me hold them in place, I will set a few stitches to fix them on the crown."

Isabel dutifully followed directions. "The ribbons are very pretty, Caroline. But the roses were beautiful. How could you just rip them off?"

"I wanted something different." Caroline pursed her lips as she concentrated on her needle. This was hardly the time to relate her discussion with Thomas regarding the artificiality of Society, and she was not sure that Isabel would agree anyway. At last, she knotted the thread and snipped it off.

Holding up the bonnet, Caroline assessed her handiwork.

"I think you were entirely successful. It is certainly different," Isabel declared.

"Do not say another word, Isabel. Everyone in London wears roses on their bonnets. I prefer being different!"

"Come, girls," Lady Clarissa called from the hallway. "The carriage is here."

The afternoon was mild and her new ribbons fluttered gaily in the gentle breeze as they headed for Whitehall. Caroline's new hyacinth carriage dress was summer weight, just another reminder of the passing weeks. Dressed in pale green with a brightly striped parasol, Isabel was fresh and excited, anxious to see the Abbey and thrilled to be facing the evening's great adventure, while Caroline anticipated the evening with very bittersweet thoughts of the impending conclusion of the Season.

When they stopped before the Abbey, Caroline felt dwarfed by the high white towers that seemed to scrape the sky. But firmly on the ground stood Lord Longbury, waiting as they climbed down from the carriage. The Langham's equipage arrived with the other members of the party and, routine pleasantries taken care of, he began his commentary. Lady Clarissa, on Count Lagerstrom's arm, and Louisa Langham, accompanied by Captain Ogden, moved close to listen.

"Other than these fine twin towers designed by Hawksmoor about sixty years ago, the Abbey building was finished in the mid-sixteenth century. Of course, they are constantly making repairs and adding monuments inside, as we shall see." Lord Longbury made a sweeping gesture toward the west front, then took Caroline's arm, half stumbling as he turned to lead the party inside.

Caroline steadied him and stifled a grin. "Careful, my lord."

"Of course, my dear, of course," he responded. "And, please, call me Gilbert."

Without waiting for an answer, Lord Longbury continued to speak as he and Caroline led the procession of five couples, Ned with Louisa's mother and Isabel with Simon bringing up the rear.

"Some say the Abbey is built on the site of a Roman temple of Apollo and later a shrine to the pagan god Thunor . . ."

Walking from the bright sunlight into the cool dimness of the vast nave, Caroline shivered, not at the change in temperature but at the absolute transformation in the atmosphere around her. She stared at the vast columns leading her eye to the soaring roof overhead, where the ribwork met in intricate patterns. Though she could hear the distant echoing of a choir practicing, the silence seemed profound. From behind them the sunlight shone through a vast stained-glass window, making gem-colored designs on the sober gray floor.

Gilbert spoke in hushed tones. "Legend has it that the first Christian church here, in the sixth century, was consecrated by

Saint Peter himself in a blaze of supernatural light accompanied by an angel choir. The Abbey has been the site of every coronation since the Norman invasion . . ."

Without actually ceasing to listen, Caroline looked over at Miss Langham and Captain Ogden. Thomas whispered something to Louisa, probably a humorous quip of some kind, knowing Thomas. Louisa's dubious look demonstrated her lack of understanding. She was a very literal person, not one with whom Thomas could share much clever repartee.

Thomas looked up to catch Caroline's eye, made a little shrug, and gave a wry smile.

Caroline was fond of Miss Langham. Louisa, gentle and quiet, wanted many children, and she was more interested in holding classes for country girls at the parish church than in the affectations of Society. She was a perfect wife for a man who would be a leader in his district. Then why, Caroline asked herself, was she so reluctant to encourage Thomas to make his offer for Louisa? If Louisa was the best choice of the Suitables, with her fortune and her sweet disposition, then Caroline ought to tell him not to wait. That was what she ought to do, but she could not.

Not yet. Not ever.

The party moved deeper into the Abbey's vastness, Lord Longbury providing details about the width of the transepts and the era of each magnificent window. Isabel and Caroline dropped back a step or two behind the others.

"Is everything ready for tonight?" Isabel asked.

"Yes. Thomas and Simon will meet us behind the mews at ten. Will should have the carriage ready."

"How can I think about flying buttresses when I am so impatient for tonight to arrive? All I can think of is sneaking out of the house. What if I drop something, like that wooden shepherdess crook, and it makes a terrible clatter?"

"You have never been clumsy in your life, Isabel. When we get home, we will have Peg take the costumes outside and hide them in the mews. Then you will not have anything to drop."

"You mean we will change in the carriage?"

"Better than having some starchy footman see me in my gypsy rags. Peg will help us."

"You mean she is coming too?"

"She has her own little plan. She and

Will can have the soft cushions of the carriage to themselves all the time we are inside."

Isabel's astonished gasp was nearly a squeal. Both Lady Clarissa and Louisa's mother turned around to see what the commotion was.

"Shush." Caroline pushed Isabel to the front and smiled sweetly at Lord Longbury.

He had not stopped for quite some time. "The Poets' Corner goes back to Chaucer, who is buried here. But this tomb was carved long after his death."

Caroline wandered toward the memorial to Shakespeare, listening to his sonnets in her head. One of them began:

> *When in disgrace with fortune and*
> *   men's eyes,*
> *I all alone beweep my outcast state,*
> *and trouble deaf heaven with my*
> *   bootless cries*
> *and look upon myself and curse my fate . . .*

Perhaps a bit theatrical as a description of her own dilemma, but not all that far off.

Thomas gazed at the tangle of marble sculptures, his eyes a little sad, every bit as imprisoned as she — though once the marriage vows were made, he could break his with little censure from the world. Had he not said, and often, that he would find his pleasure beyond the marriage bed?

Unfair. Life was unfair, especially for a woman. What chance would she have to enjoy love? Not with Lord Longbury, though he seemed to be Caroline's only choice for the present. If she gave him the tiniest encouragement, he would probably speak to Sir Barnaby when he and Aunt Augusta returned. Though Caroline did not take him in dislike, she could not begin to see herself as Lady Longbury. A future of wandering through village churches and great cathedrals listening to him drone on about Norman Perpendicular and Carolingian baroque? It was dreary beyond anything.

Caroline knew Longbury was looking for a wife to pursue his family responsibilities. His sister was married to a London dandy, and poor Gilbert could not bear to think of his family's legacy in the hands of the fribble's offspring.

Then there was Sir Reginald. He would make few demands outside the marriage bed, Caroline surmised, as long as she provided the anticipated number of offspring.

Would that be two? Or, horrors, ten?

Caroline sighed and looked at the group surrounding Lord Longbury. Miss Langham was a willing listener to every little lecture he delivered, concentrating on each marble sarcophagus, on each pane of the glorious windows, on each bronze plaque. Captain Ogden stood beside her, his face impassive, no doubt bored beyond tolerance.

Had he tried to kiss Louisa, Caroline wondered. Would Louisa have felt those velvety lips? His fiery caress? Had she run her fingers through his hair or rearranged the curls that fell across his forehead?

As if he read her thoughts, Thomas ran a hand through his hair and raised his eyes to the ancient stained-glass window above him. His face was bathed in a rose-gold glow, and in that instant, Caroline thought her heart would shatter. How could she endure without him? His every touch was fresh, his every word clear. In her dreams, in every thought, the vision of Thomas taking her in his arms overshadowed all others. Her imagination had taken them deep into the realm of passion, far beyond her experience, to a place governed by a hunger she knew nothing about but desperately desired.

Then they moved on, out of the light, but the warmth remained deep within her innermost being. Slowly Caroline walked along with the others, her mind far away, imagining the masquerade and opportunity to be in Thomas's arms. They might find a romantic trysting place, alone in the moonlit garden. In the darkness, he would kiss her, perhaps for the last time. She must savor every delight, to treasure in her memory forever.

Thomas's voice abruptly broke into her thoughts. "Here is a noble pursuit, worthy of your future."

If only he knew. "Sorry, I was woolgathering."

"Better than any seamstress or companion, Miss Parker. Here lie two queens, Mary Tudor and Elizabeth. Perhaps we might raise an army and set you up as our sovereign." He swept off an imaginary hat and bowed low. "All Hail Queen Caroline. You see, even your name is perfect. What good Englishman would not gladly trade the mad old king and his strutting son for a noble queen like Bess here?"

Caroline giggled despite herself. "How did you know that was exactly what I was thinking about? Queen, do you say?" She peered at the carved marble face on the shadowy tomb. "The virgin queen, I believe."

"Devil take it, I forgot about that part."

"At least I would not have to seek wealthy suitors. And, Sir Thomas, you can be my master of the horse."

"I live only to serve you, your majesty."

Absurdities aside, Caroline felt her throat tighten and tears well into her eyes. How fervently she wished it could be true.

Lord Longbury droned on. "The chapel of Henry the Seventh is particularly renowned for its fan vaulting."

Caroline looked upward, brushing the tears away. Far above, the stonework looked as intricate as delicate handmade lace. She tried to think of the stonemasons working all those centuries ago, but it did not help.

Thomas looked upward, then lowered his voice to a whisper. "Are you enjoying Gilbert's lessons?"

She must have looked so surprised that Thomas broke into a broad smile. "I see, Caro!"

"He is very knowledgeable."

"But pedantic and dull. Not exactly prime marriage material for a lively girl like you."

Her words came out in a plaintive tone.

"I wish I had an alternative."

Thomas drew her away from the group. "Old Reginald is not such a bad fellow. He knows more than he lets on. Has some very interesting experiments under way for his grain crops."

"I might agree, if he was at all interested in my ponies. But Sir Reginald actually told me he thought they were frivolous and a waste of feed for Uncle Jeremy."

"The fellow does lack finesse, that I will give you. But he has some fine racing bloodstock, they say."

"Perhaps if I become one of his broodmares, I could bring him round to a different view." Caroline could see Thomas bristle at her remark.

"Deuce take it, Caroline, that sounds foul. I know we have used that jargon before, but now . . ."

He exactly expressed Caroline's own feelings. It had once been a joke, the analogy to horse breeding, but now it was all too close to be funny.

Lord Longbury reassembled the group to view the coronation chair. "For more than five hundred years . . . a piece of the Stone of Scone from Scotland . . ."

Caroline knew she ought to admire the ancient chair, but in her present state of mind, she could only conclude it looked surprisingly shabby.

"Edward the First brought it to London . . ."

Caroline glanced at her mother and managed a weak grin. Lady Clarissa's look of concern brightened. For the rest of the tour, Caroline kept a smile pasted on her face. This was not the day to have her mother anxious and hovering.

At last they left the Abbey and effusively thanked Lord Longbury.

Thomas moved next to Caroline and Isabel. "Until tonight."

"My costume . . ." Isabel began.

Caroline grabbed Isabel by the arm, pulling her toward the street. "This is not the place or time to discuss our plans," Caroline murmured. She waved at Thomas, who winked as he helped Louisa climb into her carriage.

Only as they got under way did Caroline recall the final lines to the Shakespeare sonnet:

Haply I think on thee . . .
For thy sweet love remembered such wealth
  brings,
that then I scorn to change my state
  with Kings.

"I am eager to hear of your afternoon," Lady Elizabeth said.

"Our friend Lord Longbury is either an expert or tells a quick tale. He had an answer for every question anyone devised." Thomas accepted a cup of tea from his mother and sat on the saffron settee in the drawing room of Pemstead House. He had escorted Miss Langham and her mother to their home, with Ned and Simon trailing along. The two younger men had remained at the Langhams' when Thomas returned Lady Elizabeth's carriage.

"Go on." Lady Elizabeth took a delicate sip.

"Miss Langham said little. Her mother was quiet, as well."

"And?"

Thomas breathed deeply. He knew his mother would be disappointed. "I find considering her as a wife defies logic."

Lady Elizabeth sighed. "You are eliminating three perfectly suitable young women, all three with excellent fortunes? Perhaps you intend to follow Josh to Somerset, live in a stone cottage, and hoe a turnip patch?"

"Frankly, a bit of turnip cultivation doesn't sound bad. I cannot blame you for despairing of me, Mother. When I think of the marquess and the tenants who were neglected for years, I want to help. You know I never saw myself as a farmer, caring about the weather and the markets, attending fairs to exhibit prize livestock. In the last few months, I have found myself actually reading treatises on crop rotation and looking for information on disease-resistant strains of cattle."

"To be sure, Thomas, I am not surprised. Perhaps a few of your childhood experiences at Pemstead made an impression after all. Philip Ogden was not a farmer, but he saw to it that Lionel was well schooled in his responsibilities. You and Simon usually tagged along." The mention of her second husband brought a faraway, dreamy look to his mother's face.

"I fear my interest in the estate and my lack of interest in the three heiresses are both strongly felt."

"You truly believe you could never love one of them?" Lady Elizabeth sighed and lowered her eyes.

"I am afraid the prospect is not favorable."

"I am a poor adviser on love, Thomas. My first marriage to Lord Pemstead was arranged. We rubbed along tolerably well, and I believe I was gradually growing in affection for him. He did not live long, though at least he fathered a son. Lionel has had the title since he was an infant."

Thomas hugged his mother and handed her his handkerchief.

When she had wiped her eyes, she patted his knee. "This is a conversation we should have had long ago. Of course, Philip had no idea you might become Lord Aldonhurst's heir. He used to speak fondly of the old man, but the marquess's eccentricities were legendary even in Philip's youth."

She took a deep breath and smiled at Thomas. "You hardly knew your father. He was a wonderful man. I almost did not marry him because I could not imagine he would want to take on a wife with a tiny son who had a handsome title and fortune. But I fell deeply in love with Philip. He doted on Lionel, then later on you and Simon as well. I hope you have happy memories of him, because he loved you very much."

Lady Elizabeth was clearly in a reminiscent mood. She had a faraway look as she spoke. "Philip had no prospects to speak of. People thought I was daft. But I never thought twice when he asked me to be his wife. I adored him, and I still miss him terribly."

Thomas had not pictured his mother, so proper and charming, as having a great passion. Yet her eyes told the story, as though she was remembering . . . perhaps a moment of particular intensity.

Lady Elizabeth dabbed her eyes again, then cleared her throat. "Louisa seems a sweet girl. Give yourself a bit more time. See if you might not learn to love her, Thomas."

As he walked toward his club, he thought about the conversation with his mother. Surprisingly, Lady Elizabeth seemed to be a romantic. She was correct to think of Miss Langham as sweet, but how could he live with Louisa? He could not remember what she wore earlier in the afternoon, even how much of her face he could see beneath the bonnet. A few nights ago when she sang, she was . . . the only image that came into his mind was Caroline with her golden curls and wide smile.

Ah, Caroline. He was besotted with her. How could he have let such a thing happen? In the past, he had been so careful. He really had believed he could do without love. A few dalliances with lightskirts and several flirtations with married ladies last Season had been promising, though he never followed up on the invitations.

And now he was as skewered as the most fervent recipient of Cupid's darts. Bold measures were called for to rid himself of the affliction.

But they would have to wait. Tonight, incognito, he and Caroline would have a few moments of stolen pleasure. Those minutes would be the most precious of his life.

Fourteen

"Avast, me pretties." Thomas wore a black mask over his eyes and a white silk shirt with full balloon sleeves. "Don't gawk like the green girls ye are or ye'll be found out."

Caroline could not help staring, not only at Thomas, a delicious sight. The streets near the Brevort mansion were jammed with high-strung horses pulling coaches filled with merry revelers who spilled out of their carriages, laughing loudly and shouting to each other. One outlandish costume crowded after another through the patches of bright light and dark shadows cast by dozens of blazing flambeaux. Colorful harlequins, fierce Vikings in horned helmets, and Greek goddesses in diaphanous draperies mixed with Celtic barbarians brandishing wooden shields and swords, devils with red pointed tails and long sharp forks, and a druid priest escorting a Spanish dancer. The many in dark, faintly menacing dominoes reminded Caroline of some kind of evil, hooded executioners.

Isabel's eyes were wide with excitement, and Caroline feared Thomas's admonition was all too fitting. In their state of high excitement, both girls must be gaping like the country cabbage heads they were.

"I've never seen anything like it." Isabel sounded quite breathless.

"This is what you wanted." Simon laughed at their reactions.

"Ladies, I think we'll make faster progress to the door if we leave the carriage here." Thomas rapped on the roof.

Leaving Peg alone inside, they climbed out of the coach. "We'll find you around Grosvenor Square, Will," Thomas called as the two couples linked arms and merged into the stream of characters making their way toward regal heralds flanking the steps of the Brevorts' stately town house.

"One would have to say this is quite definitely the less proper branch of London's Society," Thomas remarked as they passed an eye-filling nymph wearing only a few filmy scarves.

Isabel's eyes were once more wide as saucers. "Caroline! That gown was completely transparent."

Caroline giggled. "If one could call it a gown at all."

Simon waved a hand in the air. "Cer-

297

tainly is a good thing it is a warm night."

Swept along in the throng, they soon found themselves inside the vast hall, still in the middle of a crowd every bit as rowdy as the mob outside.

Caroline was pleased to see their costumes were unremarkable. The last thing they needed was to draw the attention of anyone who might recognize them. As a shepherdess, Isabel's outfit followed a familiar and popular theme. Caroline had covered her own head with a gypsy shawl and wore a ragged skirt, with bright baubles and scarves wound around her neck and layers of bangles on her wrists. Both wore masks to shield most of their faces.

Caroline found the music loud and boisterous, the laughter doubly so. Making their way through the crush, she saw an eighteenth-century Madame Pompadour with a towering powdered wig and wide hoop skirt. As she looked, a man grabbed the bottom hoop and raised it over his head, bringing make-believe shrieks from the lady and causing raucous cheers from onlookers as he disappeared under the voluminous skirt.

"Oh my, my!" The Pompadour wiggled as if in the throes of delight. "You have a quarter hour to stop that!"

Thomas grabbed Caroline and jerked her forward after Isabel and Simon. "This is no place for the likes of you."

Caroline was far more shocked than she would ever admit. "Do not be silly. We gypsies are quite worldly."

Colorful characters jammed the rooms in a mixture of eras and auras that made Caroline's head spin. Cleopatra leaned across a Chinese mandarin to embrace a glittering angel cloaked head to toe in silvery gauze. The clanking of a knight's armor and the silvery bells of a harem dancer punctuated blaring laughter, boisterous shrieks, and bellowing shouts.

Slowly Caroline and Thomas moved among the bodies packed shoulder to shoulder until they could hear the orchestra tuning up to begin another set.

Caroline put her mouth close to Thomas's ear. "We seem to have lost Simon and Isabel."

"No telling where they could be in this crush."

"I doubt the disappearance was accidental. We should find them."

"Do not worry, Caro. Simon will protect her if she needs it."

"I hope you are right."

Caroline looked into his eyes, and in the

midst of the noisy crowd, their gazes locked. The tumult silenced. All she felt, heard, and saw was her yearning ache, raw and real. She was warm all over, not from the temperature but from a different kind of heat. Buried inside her a sensation she could not describe in words grew more intense, softening every nerve, spreading to her fingertips.

Nothing else mattered. Only here. Only now. Only Thomas.

As if they were alone, Thomas bent to brush his lips across hers, and she trembled in delight. She paid no heed to the clanging of her bracelets as she placed her hands on his chest and slowly inched her fingers upward until her arms wrapped around his neck. Her ears filled with his little purrs of pleasure as he clamped his body to hers.

Around them the revelry swirled, the dancers began to revolve, and the earth spun. Between them a pair of formerly hesitant sparks flared into a blaze that fused them together.

When they broke apart, Caroline had to wipe tears from her cheeks, though she was not crying. Thomas grabbed two goblets from a passing footman and handed one to her. The champagne had a tickling coolness and a refreshingly tart flavor. Slowly the room, the jam of people, the sound of the orchestra beginning a waltz, all their surroundings began to come into focus again.

Thomas guided her to the fringes of the room where they set down their glasses. His face wore a melancholy look, a sadness, a difference she could not explain.

Half the people on the floor were not even trying to dance but stood and conversed while others moved slowly around them. Wordlessly, she moved into his waiting arms, and they began to sway to the cadence of the music, hardly moving because of the crush.

Caroline almost expected Thomas to make a humorous quip, but his eyes remained glued to her face, his lips curved in a partial smile, a smile with intriguing overtones. He was neither in a teasing mood, nor jolly and carefree, a new Thomas she felt she had known for a long time without realizing. The pulsing rhythm of the music and the sensation of her breasts pressing against his warm, hard chest caused her conscious thoughts to vanish, consumed by the exhilaration of his embrace.

Through open terrace doors, the dancers

spilled out of the warm ballroom onto the dark stone veranda. The magic of the night, the sheltering anonymity, the aloneness in the midst of hundreds was as intoxicating as the wine.

To the orchestra's lilting strains, Thomas held her in his arms and slowly circled the terrace. This was the moment, Caroline thought, the moment she had been waiting for, the moment she had risked so much to achieve. Her heart thundered as slowly they twirled to the darkest part of the terrace where he stopped dancing, bringing her body close to his from toe to lips. He kissed her, caressing her shoulders and running his fingers through her free-flowing hair.

"My God, Caro. Why? Why?"

She easily read his thoughts, for they mirrored her own. Why must either endure a loveless marriage? Her heart soared, for she suspected now he truly loved her. But the situation was impossible. They both knew that, too.

"Thomas? Can we forget everything else tonight and just pretend?"

"I do not need to pretend, Caro, my darling. This is real." He tightened his arms around her, nuzzling her shoulder and neck.

She laughed, and he joined in briefly, then claimed her lips again. The kiss was magical, and Caroline knew she was not pretending, either.

They broke apart and strolled deeper into the garden, deeper into the darkness. They were silent, each reflecting on their thoughts. Shadowy figures entwined in complicated postures possessed the benches and secluded themselves behind the statuary. Caroline could hear their low voices, an occasional gasping snicker.

A couple moved off a bench in a secluded alcove and Thomas led her to the seat. They kissed again and he pushed the thin blouse off her shoulder, caressing her bare skin. She wanted him to touch her everywhere as her breath quickened with needs that flowed from a desire she had never known. When his fingertips reached the tip of her breast, she gasped in surprise, surprise at his boldness, surprise at the bolt of lightning that slammed through her.

"Just think of me as a marauding pirate, my darling."

"Gypsy girls are known to be fast."

"And passionate."

Caroline could not describe the waves of heat and abandon that swept through her.

She was being devoured by an uncontrol-
lable force. Through the heat and roar in
her ears, she could hear him murmur, then
felt him move away.

They could hear another couple on the
other side of the shrubbery, and the voices
sounded all too familiar.

"Oh, David, I am tortured by waiting."

"I want you, Clarissa. Now."

"Just a few more weeks, darling. I know
Caroline has resisted, but I am sure she
will accept an offer very soon. Then, when
we are together in Vienna, my dear,
nothing will ever part us again."

Caroline shivered, abruptly cold, as
though enveloped in a chill shroud. She
wanted to scream, to run away, to hide.
She understood it all now, the rush for her
come out, for her marriage. Oh, everything
was all too clear. Her thundering heartbeat
continued to pound, but now it had the cadence of doom.

She pulled out of Thomas's arms, and he
let her go without comment.

Slowly and without a word they crept
away and returned to the ballroom. Caroline trembled and tears threatened to burst
out at any moment. How could her mother
have done this to her? And yet, she
thought, perhaps Clarissa was justified.

She had been a faithful wife, and now she was prevented from marrying the count, though she loved him. Her mother had never lied, just neglected the most important part of the count's story.

She, Caroline, held the key to her mother's happiness. If she refused to marry this Season, her mother would not go to Vienna with David. If Caro indulged her desire to discourage all offers, she condemned her mother to unhappiness.

Almost unconsciously, Caroline and Thomas walked back through the house and out the front door, without speaking, without even noticing the revelers except as impediments to rapid progress. The streets had quieted now, lined by waiting coaches.

"We cannot go back to the carriage yet. We would interrupt Peg and Will."

"Here." Thomas gestured to the well-scrubbed steps of a nearby mansion fronting the street. "We can sit here on the steps for a while. No telling how long Isabel and Simon will stay at the ball."

"I have lost all sense of time." Caroline sighed and occupied herself in rearranging her shawls.

"Are you catching a chill?"

"Not at all."

For some time they sat in uncomfortable silence. She kept her eyes on her hands, twisting her necklaces and from time to time giving a whimpery sigh.

When she shivered again, Thomas slipped his arm about her shoulder, pulling her close.

Caroline sniffed. "I wish Mama had confided in me. Now I understand, but perhaps if I had known the whole story earlier, we could have worked it out another way."

"I am afraid I do not understand anything." Thomas sounded confused and sad.

Caroline took his hand and lovingly caressed it. "This is the reason Mama wants me to marry. She wants to be with the count, to live with him in Vienna."

"That much I do understand."

"He is married. His wife is sick and demented. She will spend her life as an invalid."

"Ah, that explains quite a lot, but not why you must make a match."

"Mama knows she will be ruined if she lives with the count. I guess she thinks if she can have me safely married, I will not share her ruin in Society."

"And we can safely assume Lady Augusta knows nothing?"

"I am certain Aunt Augusta is quite in the dark. But, you see, I do not care a fig for what Society thinks. Though I never suspected Mama's motives, I have tried to tell her again and again that I am more than happy to remove myself from all this town nonsense and rusticate forever."

"But she is concerned with your future well-being."

"Yes. I have a small legacy from Papa, just a few hundred pounds a year. But no matter how I argue my case, she is determined that I find a wealthy match."

"But if you do not?"

"Her happiness is at stake. She will not go with David to Vienna unless I am married."

"And if you refuse?"

"I cannot refuse. I could never forgive myself if I spoiled her chances for love."

"What about your happiness?"

"She has always said that love can grow after marriage. How many people ever find love? You, Thomas Ogden, will not marry for love. You say you do not even believe in love."

He stared into the distance. "So which of the Eligibles will you choose? Is the lucky fellow Lord Longwinded? Or will Reg the Veg receive the nod?"

In spite of herself, Caroline giggled. "You are merciless. Now I have to ask you the same question. Will you offer for the indescribably wealthy Maria, the loquacious Georgina, or timid Louisa?"

He heaved a great sigh. "Of the three, only Louisa is near tolerable. Between your two, Sir Reggie is by far more likely to turn up his toes soon."

Astonished, she stared at him openmouthed. Then he saw a mischievous look steal into her eye. With a crafty smile, she feigned a thoughtful expression. "The way Gilbert stumbles about, he is likely to trip over a headstone in some churchyard and break his neck."

Thomas matched her shifty tone. "And might we just help the dear boy along?"

Their laughter was short-lived, and again a melancholy mood saddened his features.

Thomas sighed again. "Too bad I am not a real pirate, or a highwayman. Then I could end our predicament."

"Or," she declared, brightening again, "if I were really a gypsy, I could pick a few pockets, the right pockets."

Again they sat in gloomy silence, lost in thought. For the thousandth time, Caroline twisted the beads around her fingers. Her mother deserved her happiness with

Count Lagerstrom. All other decisions hung on that fact.

A crowd of rowdy knights and their ladies progressed along the street, calling unintelligible wine-soaked insults to one another, then hooting with laughter. When their noise faded, Caroline watched a cluster of coachmen at the corner, crouching low, probably over a dice game. Empty coaches lined the street, horses dozing in the dark.

"Thomas? Would you do something for me?"

"Of course, Caro. Anything."

She kept her eyes on the horses across the way. Now that she was prepared to ask, she felt a wave of fear. "This is very important to me."

"Caroline, I . . . I will do anything you ask."

"Will you take the ponies? I cannot bear to sell them to the countess. And when I marry, I will not have enough time. Neither Sir Reginald nor Lord Longbury would want them around, and I could not bear to neglect them. Perhaps at Aldonhurst you would have a place. And you might even continue to breed ponies. Many people have been interested." She ran out of breath and stared down at her hands, all shackled in ropes of beads.

"Are you certain you do not want to keep the four, Caroline?"

"Yes. I could not endure having them nearby and neglecting them." Caroline fought off her tears.

"Then I shall buy them from you."

"No! I told you, the ponies are not for sale. They are a gift in exchange for your promise to care for them. That is all. I refuse to consider any other course."

"So this Queen Elizabeth business has taken hold?"

Caroline could not help smiling. Thomas and his sly wit. He could never let a serious moment take root. How she would miss his shrewd humor. "Absolutely. Be careful or I will send you to the Tower."

More people walked down the steps of the Brevorts'. The party was drawing to a close. Soon Simon and Isabel would come along on their way to their rendezvous with the carriage. Caroline heaved a great sigh.

Thomas looked up, and she read a soft sympathy in his eyes. Her lips tingled and every nerve in her body thrust her forward into his arms. She felt his hands on her back, fitting her to him with exquisitely defined exactness. His mouth was warm and wet, and she opened hers with a helpless moan.

The touch of his gentle fingers on her neck and in her hair awoke appetites she hardly knew existed. In her imagination, she was being swept off to an enchanted realm where nothing mattered but his powerful caresses and her craving for more and more. Again and again, they kissed, trailing their lips to forehead, hairline, cheeks, and chin. Her inhibitions gone, she drew his hand to her breast, glorying in the fiery sensations that sparked through the fragile layer of silk.

His kiss, deep and pulsing, and his body heavy on hers pressed her against the steps. Still, she wanted more, more of some primal desire she could not name but to which she surrendered fully. Her hands clutched at his shoulders, pulling him yet closer.

Abruptly he yanked himself away. "We must stop, Caro. Save your wanton urges for your husband." He propped his elbow on his knee and hid his face in his hand.

Stunned, Caroline fought to control her ragged breath. "What did you say?"

"I said we must stop. There is no use torturing ourselves. You and I cannot afford to play at love."

"But, Thomas, I do not understand . . ."

"No one understands. Love or lust, what is the difference? You are fortunate, Caroline. You have strong feelings. You will enjoy bedding your husband. Many women never enjoy it, or so I hear, for my experience would not support such a theory."

His words were so painful she wished she could close her ears. But every word resounded in her consciousness. "But, Thomas, I know nothing . . ."

He interrupted again. "Girls of your class, Caroline, spend most of their young lives being taught to repress their emotions, to deny the cravings of their bodies. Is it any wonder then, that their men find them lamentably dull? Such females may be valuable for breeding, but for pleasure, men can find it with other types of . . ."

"Stop!" she cried. "I cannot listen to another word."

Caroline blew her nose on a ragged strip from her skirt and stole a peek at Thomas. Unless she was entirely mistaken, his face sagged in misery, not just weariness. Her initial horror at his uncalled-for commentary had already begun to fade. Men apparently had all sorts of rationalizations for their own weaknesses. If she was convinced he was entirely sincere, she would give him a strong piece of her mind, and she could think of a number of phrases that would fit. But a bit of doubt remained. His kisses seemed to have far more sincerity than his words.

Thomas let himself into his silent, darkened rooms. He had some heavy-duty drinking to do, and he wanted no more company. He raised the bottle to his lips and took a long draught, splattering a few drops on his tattered pirate shirt, then wiping his mouth with the back of his hand.

This was not his first bottle since he had seen the young ladies home, Caroline morose and silent, Isabel tipsy and giggling. Simon had also consumed enough of the Brevort champagne to make him a useless drinking partner. Thomas hoped Simon had managed the stairs at Pemstead House without waking all the servants and Lady Elizabeth, too. Now, having been turned out of his club with the last of the stragglers, Thomas sought solace in a last bottle of brandy.

He wanted to get totally starched, completely senseless, but somehow he only became more and more despondent. Each gloomy thought intruded on another, worsening his depression, deepening his misery. What he said to Caroline had been cruel and disgusting. He hoped she would never think kindly of him again.

Had he not stolen every kind of innocence from her? First, his desperate desire to make love to her had steered them to that dark garden, where she discovered her mother's motives. Better if she had never known the real reason Lady Clarissa wanted her daughter settled. Caroline's adoration and admiration of her mother had been perfect and complete. Now she was ready to sacrifice her own happiness, marry someone she could not love, all for her mother's sake.

But worse, Caroline had lost her innocence about passion. Though far from consummated, Thomas knew their embraces had engendered feelings and physical reactions she had never experienced. Now he had given her a taste of love and passion together. By indulging his own desires, he condemned her to a double penance: she would marry without love but knowing what desire felt like, what deep emotions could bring to the physical relationship between a man and a woman.

For that matter, what had he done to

himself? He had learned the same lesson, too. He had lost his heart to Caroline, but he would wed another. And forevermore, he would fulfill his lusts in the arms of women he did not love but merely used to satisfy his urges.

The foul things he had said to her, calling her wanton . . . he hoped she would find them unforgivable. Alone in his misery, he raised the bottle and poured more brandy down his throat.

Worst of all, Caroline had offered her ponies, giving up the most precious thing she owned. She was willing to sacrifice everything. Her independence. Her happiness. Her love.

He buried his face in his hands. He had to stop her.

Fifteen

Caroline felt dry of tears as dawn broke. Isabel slept like she had been drugged, oblivious to her cousin's long dismal hours of weeping. Alone in her bed, Caroline again and again relived the ecstatic moments with Thomas and the dreadful discovery of her mother's motives. As she danced with Thomas in her mind, Caroline felt wonderful, as if their love could accomplish miracles.

But Thomas had been speaking champagne words, not the arguments of his heart and soul. He was a charming rogue, and she had been a fool ever to consider he would abandon his search for the heiress.

Why had she fallen in love with him? After all, he had told her how he needed a rich wife, how he did not believe in love, how he would continue to enjoy his pleasures where he found them. He claimed to be rotten husband material, without a source of funds, but he had charm enough for dozens of men.

Rather a pity, she mused, for he underestimated his own character and denied his abilities, denigrated his knowledge of agriculture but spent many an hour in serious study. Poor Thomas. Was he so convinced he was shallow he did not bother to investigate his own depths?

Now their pathetic alliance, her lamentable flirtation, was over. Tomorrow she would see Uncle Jeremy's man of business and find out how to give ownership of the ponies to Thomas. They would have a good home with him, of that she was certain. Probably by next year they would reside in a newly constructed stable with the finest of accoutrements, a staff of caretakers who adored them and respected their very agreeable master, the handsome and dashing Marquess of Aldonhurst — and his most biddable wife, whose ample purse made such luxuries possible.

Thomas woke slowly, little by little conscious of the morning sounds from outside. He tried to roll over and almost toppled onto the floor, for he had fallen asleep on a narrow settee. He sat up slowly, trying to calm the pounding in his head, the pain behind his eyes, the ache across the back of his neck, the dark thoughts swirling through his brain.

Unfortunately, each detail he remembered about last night made matters worse. Caroline insisted he take her ponies, her most precious damned possession in the world. He was utterly unworthy of having even her blasted glove, much less her beloved team. He sank back, his arm across his face.

Was it only yesterday at the club he talked with Etheridge about bringing back a field's fertility by alternating crops that gave more to the soil than they took? What a joke to think he could make the estate pay unless he poured money into it.

Yet Caroline had faith in him. Why else would she give him the ponies? And he would not let her down. He and Josh could repair the roof of the stable with the help of a couple of lads from the village. There had to be a few of the locals who would work for a share in future returns, after all the years of no employment at all.

Thomas thought of the volume of notes he had at home, covering a multitude of topics from drainage schemes to enhancing egg production. The town house repairs were under way, and he was certain he could lease it out within the month. His throbbing head notwithstanding, he began to develop a trace of hope.

Many hours passed before Thomas asked his mother to accompany him in a visit to Lady Clarissa Parker that afternoon. A long soak in a hot tub, headache powders, and a few bites of beef pie helped to revive him. He wore his best jacket and buff breeches with his highly polished boots.

"I do not understand why we must call on her today," Lady Elizabeth said. "I am most fond of Lady Clarissa, but I saw her only the day before yesterday."

"My purpose will be clear once we are there." Thomas spoke quietly, taking care not to endanger his recovery. "I want you with me to explain."

"Explain what?"

The announcement of the town coach's arrival saved Thomas from replying. He helped his mother onto the deep velvet seat and took his place across from her.

Now that he had made up his mind what to do, Thomas was anxious to carry it out. His visit to her mother was timed to begin just after Caroline left to drive the ponies in the park with Isabel. At just minutes before the usual time, he had his coachman stop halfway down the block from Caroline's turn into Hyde Park.

"I wish I understood what you are up to,

Thomas. You are strangely quiet, and that is setting off all sorts of nerve-wracking thoughts in my brain."

Thomas laughed softly as he watched the street. "Do not worry, Mother. Everything will be clear in just a few minutes."

"And in the meantime, I simmer like a cauldron of soup over a fire!"

When Thomas saw Caroline's rig heading toward the gates, he tapped on the roof, and the Pemstead coach continued on to Berkeley Square.

Lady Clarissa hardly masked her surprise at receiving them, but performed all the usual observances, ordering tea and exchanging pleasantries.

Once everyone was settled, Thomas began. "I have asked my mother to accompany me here, Lady Clarissa, to discuss my forthcoming betrothal."

Lady Elizabeth straightened up in surprise. "Just yesterday you said you had few hopes of concluding an arrangement."

Thomas went on. "That is correct. But I have come to a decision. The young lady I wish to offer for is Miss Parker."

"Oh dear," Lady Clarissa breathed.

Lady Elizabeth looked befuddled. "But this is not what . . ."

Thomas interrupted her. "I love Caroline, and I believe she loves me. But before I ask for her hand, I want to be certain you will not oppose us, Lady Clarissa."

Lady Clarissa frowned and pursed her lips.

Thomas continued. "Caroline and I have tried to help each other find agreeable matches, but in the process I fear we have lost our hearts to one another instead of to our intended victims. Last night, Lady Clarissa, Caroline discovered why you are so anxious to have her settled by autumn."

"What?" Lady Clarissa's hand flew to her throat, her face draining of color.

"Be assured," Thomas said, "your secret is secure. Not even my mother knows anything about it."

Lady Elizabeth wore an uncharacteristic frown. "Thomas, can you please explain?"

"In a moment, Mother. Lady Clarissa, your daughter is very happy for you. She is determined to see that your happiness is fulfilled, no matter what the cost to her."

"Oh, no," breathed Lady Clarissa, beginning to weep.

"She told me last night she would encourage Lord Longbury and Sir Reginald. Whoever asks first, she will accept. But I cannot stand by and see her marry someone else when I believe she loves me and I love her. I regret exceedingly that I do not have a vast fortune or even a modest income capable of providing her with the comfort she richly deserves."

"You truly love her, Thomas?"

"With all my heart."

Lady Clarissa sniffed and wiped her eyes. "I know I should be happy if Caroline has found love, but she has virtually no dowry, and Thomas has . . ."

"Yes, it is true I have little in the way of funds, Lady Clarissa. But, contrary to what most people think, I actually have very impressive prospects."

"Be careful you do not exaggerate, Thomas," his mother warned. "A title means little without the means to support it."

"What title?" Clarissa asked.

Thomas smiled for the first time, amused at the tangle. "I will inherit considerable land someday. The estate, Aldonhurst, has thousands of acres. At the moment this land is empty and unproductive. But I have hired a new bailiff, and in just a short time I will join him at the estate. I intend to make the place productive again."

Now it was Lady Elizabeth's turn to be surprised. "I applaud your determination,

Thomas. But how will you do it without a large infusion of funds?"

Thomas explained to Lady Clarissa. "That was part of my pact with your daughter. We both sought a moneyed match. My wife's fortune was to have been spent on estate restoration, though I was never keen on the idea."

Lady Elizabeth bristled. "In my opinion, it would be quite the best situation."

"Ladies, this is the whole point. I believe that together, Caroline and I can bring Aldonhurst back to prosperity through our own hard work, however unfashionable that sounds. I pledge to both of you my most concerted efforts to make Caroline comfortable and content. I believe she will be a willing and enthusiastic participant in the management of the estates, beginning with the establishment of a breeding program for more carriage ponies."

Lady Clarissa ventured a tiny smile. "I believe you are determined to succeed, Thomas. And when it comes to ponies, no one is more dedicated than Caroline."

Lady Elizabeth beamed and wiped a tear from her eye. "I always knew you had the capacity for estate management, Thomas."

"May I remind you that, to this point, my ideas are untested? I have read many treatises, talked with many agricultural experts and a number of landowners. But my actual capacity to put my ideas into practice is unknown."

"But you are prepared and you are determined. I have no fear of the outcome." Lady Elizabeth punctuated her statement with emphatic nods of approval.

Thomas searched Lady Clarissa's face. "Lady Clarissa, do I have your permission to ask Caroline to marry me?"

"I hoped she could be well provided for." She turned to Lady Elizabeth. "My late husband, Sir Quentin, came from a poor branch of a noble family. He served the king all his life, but his rewards were not often monetary."

Lady Elizabeth went to Lady Clarissa and gently embraced her. "Clarissa, my dear, I do not know why you are so distraught, but if Caroline loves Thomas and he loves her, they must be together."

Thomas spoke gravely. "Some day I hope to have a fortune. Now all I have is my love."

Clarissa wiped her eyes again. "If Caroline shares your feelings, Thomas, you have my blessing. As you know, love is not an emotion I take lightly."

"And I wish you the joy of it."

"My sister Augusta will be very disappointed not to have concluded a titled match for Caroline with one of her favorites. I, of course have no such requirements, but Augusta was hoping to snag her a title of some sort, I believe."

Lady Elizabeth looked from Clarissa to Thomas and back. "Would she be satisfied with marchioness, do you think?"

Clarissa's hand flew to her throat. "Never say so! I shall have to remember to have the sherry at hand when I tell Augusta."

Lady Elizabeth stared at Thomas. "We did not want to tell anyone. The old marquess is ill and has long been a recluse."

Thomas held up a hand in warning. "Wait. I have not discussed this with Caroline yet. Do I have your assurance that if she agrees to become my wife, you will concur, Lady Clarissa?"

"With pleasure, Thomas." She embraced him. "For some weeks, I have noticed Caroline's partiality toward you. You have spent much time keeping company, and I am not surprised you have lost your hearts to one another." Giving him over to his mother's arms, Lady Clarissa added, "And I will see to it that Barnaby and Augusta approve as well."

They heard a commotion in the hall. Then Ned burst into the drawing room. "Aunt Clarissa," he exclaimed. "She said yes. She said yes!"

Suddenly looking about the room to see Thomas and Lady Elizabeth, Ned stood quite disheveled and red-faced from his rush. "Ogden," he panted, "Lady Elizabeth. Wish me happy. Miss Langham and I will marry in August."

Thomas slapped Ned's shoulder. "I hope I will not be far behind!" He rushed from the room, leaving his mother and Lady Clarissa to hear every detail of Ned's exhilarated joy.

Caroline wished the day were dark and dreary, cloudy and gloomy, with rain threatening under thunderous black clouds, instead of a bright, sunny, cloudless sky of vivid blue. Even over the jangle of the harness and the cadence of the ponies' hooves, she could hear the trill of the birds and the happy shouts of children sailing boats on the pond. And nothing Caroline said halted Isabel's chattering.

On the way to the park, Isabel nursed the effects of last night's overindulgence. But after a half hour or so of the fine, sunny fresh air, she talked continuously, detailing every moment of her adventurous evening. Isabel and Simon had sipped champagne, admired the fanciful costumes, sampled the lobster puffs and *côtelettes de veau*, and danced until their feet cried for mercy.

"I danced with many strangers. And when everyone unmasked at midnight, Simon introduced me as a refugee from France, his distant cousin now residing in far-off Yorkshire."

Caroline tried to summon a reprimand, but had no heart for it. Isabel had not even noticed how blue-deviled she and Thomas were when they met outside the Brevorts'.

Isabel paid no heed to Caroline's silence. "Peg looked very happy with her evening in the carriage with Will."

"Yes." Caroline agreed absently, deeply absorbed in her own bleak thoughts. Aunt Augusta and Sir Barnaby returned next week. The proposal for her hand that Caroline dreaded was now a necessity if her mother's plans were to prosper.

"I am sure Mama would allow Peg and Will to marry and continue to live at Sunnyslope."

Caroline was torn with indecision. Which man was preferable, Lord Longbury or Sir Reginald? They were the only two likely prospects for a timely offer for her hand. Oh, dreariest of prospects, Caroline lamented to herself.

Isabel prattled on. "We can have a lovely wedding for them at All Saints and invite the whole village."

For herself, Caroline thought, a quiet ceremony with no more than a handful of witnesses would suffice. She cringed inwardly at the thought of standing beside Gilbert, that is if he made it to the altar without stumbling . . . or Reginald, probably accompanied by his gaggle of sisters.

"We will fill the chancel with wildflowers and weave roses into Peg's hair."

Caroline tried to make a mental list of benefits and drawbacks for each man, but could make herself go no further than the simple fact that any list would be headed by her own aversion to the betrothal, to the marriage, and most definitely to the man.

"Then a huge wedding party on the lawn, with a feast and dancing under lanterns hung in the trees."

Caroline decided to cut short today's exercise before she was harassed into boxing Isabel's ears. She needed time to be alone and quiet, to sort out her thoughts.

As they turned toward the mews, Caroline was surprised to see Thomas heading toward them on foot. He waved, then bowed as she pulled the team to a stop beside him.

"Good morning, ladies. I hope you are feeling well this morning."

His grin made Caroline want to melt. Why did he not go away and stay away? When she saw him, she wanted to forgive every wicked word he had uttered.

Thomas patted Oberon's shiny neck. "If we drop Lady Isabel at Barstow House, would you take me for a bit of a jaunt, Caroline?"

"We are actually finished for the day."

"But these fellows look full of vigor and ready for more."

"Oh, we hardly did half of our usual route." Isabel spoke out of innocence.

Reluctantly, Caroline agreed to Thomas's request. Her mind was so muddled she could not think of a single excuse to put him off. Once they had dropped off Isabel at the front door, Caroline gave vent to her frustration.

"Sir, you will please make this your final visit to Barstow House this Season."

"Why, you injure me. After our caper last night, I thought we had decided to be, ah, reasonable and clearheaded about our association, Caroline. I am merely trying to be logical."

"My position is difficult enough without having you around." He had no idea how hurt she felt at his cavalier disregard of her situation. How easily he had cast aside his feelings and assumed this mantle of sophisticated indifference.

"I need your assistance. I have decided to whom I will offer marriage."

Caroline wanted to shove him off the curricle seat, preferably into an immense pile of drayhorse droppings, but none was handy.

When she said nothing, he went on. "You do not congratulate me? I thought you might be well pleased that our scheme has come to fruition."

Blown up is more the way I see it, she wanted to say. Blown right up in our faces.

"My problem is this, Caroline —"

"If you are going to become a married man, Captain Ogden, perhaps you should return to addressing me less familiarly. Miss Parker will do very nicely to command my attention."

Thomas rubbed his hand across his mouth, noisily clearing his throat and coughing into his handkerchief.

Maybe, she prayed, he was choking. The way his eyes were watering and his face had turned red, he looked like he was strangling. She could not think of any better candidate to wish a severe case of apoplexy.

When he recovered his aplomb, he cleared his throat once more. "You see, I wish to have your help in deciding the choice of a proper time and place for the proposal. I feel a most romantic setting is called for, an extraordinary location where we can be alone."

You harebrained popinjay, she wanted to shout. You hardly need to be alone to act romantic. You kissed me in the middle of a crowd of strangers, bufflehead. Instead, she said, "I would suggest a quiet garden at twilight, or perhaps a spot with lovely vistas over the city on Hampstead Heath."

Caroline wondered how a person went about hiring the services of a shrewd footpad or a notorious highwayman to give him the kind of fright he deserved.

"Then you would recommend an outdoor setting. But what if the skies do not cooperate? No, I think I shall need to concoct a stratagem to get the young lady alone while indoors."

You have not had any trouble finding methods in my case, she thought, feeling her anger fading into anguish.

"Then again, at a ball," he went on, "if one searches for an empty salon, one is apt to disturb another couple stealing a private moment, and such a fumble hardly seems conducive to the appropriate mood."

"Obviously His Majesty lost an eminent military strategist when you left the army, Captain Ogden."

Again seized with a choking spell, Thomas covered his face with a handkerchief.

When he recovered, his voice was shaky. "You would say, I take it, that I am making too big a thing of it?"

"By no means," she answered sarcastically. "Just because you will hire the King's trumpeters and a string symphony . . ."

"Music! The perfect background. Now where could I put an orchestra?"

"Why not call on Prinny and see if he will loan you Carlton House for an evening?"

For a third time, Thomas was consumed by a hacking cough.

Caroline showed not an iota of sympathy. "If you have caught a chill, I suggest you postpone your plan until you have made a full recovery. Your intended is not likely to find these spasms any more appealing than I do."

"I beg your pardon, Miss Parker." Thomas choked out his apology. "Perhaps you will bring the team to a stop and I will try to restore myself."

"Whoa!" Caroline gently reined in the ponies.

Suddenly without throat problems, Thomas spoke easily. "Perhaps it will come as no surprise for you to know I have been teasing you."

She frowned in bewilderment. "About what?"

"The format for my proposal. Actually, I am in need of no assistance."

Her frown deepened.

Thomas smiled. "I choose this place and this time. Caroline, I want you to be my wife."

"What? Your wife?" His sudden switch in mood left her mind baffled. All she could think of were his warnings against belief in love. "Do you think I would marry you instead of one of the others and then share you with some lightskirt? I would never stand by and let you wander off into any bedroom you wish. Or take lovers myself while you philander. How dare you insult me with an offer of marriage!"

Thomas reached for her hand, but she

snatched it away. "Caroline, please wait!"

She hardly stopped for breath before launching another tirade. "You are the most conceited, self-centered, arrogant, and foolish quiz I have ever had the misfortune to encounter. You have no respect for females whatsoever. You think you can simply cast a girl one of those toad-eating smiles and any chit you wink at will fall into your clutches. You are a miserable, hypocritical cur, Thomas Ogden. And . . . and you can go to the devil!" She dissolved into tears, dropping the reins and burying her face in her hands. The ponies, well trained, did not stir.

"Has your sermon concluded?"

His question renewed her invective. "No, it has not! If you had an ounce of integrity, you would know that an honorable person like me would never ally herself with a heartless rake with no respect for marriage vows. In fact, I cannot imagine why I never told the Suitables exactly what your views are."

When she looked into his grin, her anger reflamed. "Don't you dare laugh, you contemptible scoundrel!"

Thomas secured the reins and climbed out of the phaeton, lifting a helpless Caroline and setting her on the grass beside the path, where she sank to her knees. Tears wet her cheeks and dripped onto her lap.

Thomas put his arm around her and sat down, pulling her close. "Wait, my precious love. I have been talking such nonsense for so long I never realized you still believed that rubbish about not believing in marriage vows. Can you listen to me for a moment?"

She nodded, keeping her eyes lowered.

"Last night I felt quite desperate. I have been trying not to admit to myself that I have fallen completely in love. Yes, the same Thomas that scoffed at the very existence of love is now the eagerest apostle of Cupid's mania. I want to spend the rest of my life with you beside me, Caroline."

She could hardly believe her ears. Caroline's heartbeat adjusted its tempo from anger to a growing exhilaration.

"I am sorry about teasing you. When I asked you to help me choose a setting for a proposal I expected you to ask, 'To whom?' and I was ready to negotiate a new alliance between us."

"I was already quite out of sorts. Contemplating marriage with the Eligibles put me in the sullens."

"I have already secured your mother's blessing, Caro."

Caroline smiled, her eyes still bright with tears. "You have? I should not be so missish."

"I misjudged your mood entirely, my darling. You know our life will not be easy. I know we can build Aldonhurst up to its former status, but the process will be long and difficult. We will have many years before we reach financial success."

"I have never wanted any life other than to live in the country. I know I will love Aldonhurst."

He leaned closer, but she stopped him with her palm pressed in the center of his chest. "Are you serious about believing in love?"

He grasped her hand in his and held it in place. "I swear it. And I promise you I will give up all my bad habits."

"Including any thoughts of . . ."

"I pledge eternal obedience to all the marriage vows, to the letter."

Caroline smiled through her tears. "Thomas, I believe you."

The pony Oberon nodded his dark head, jingling the bit and rattling the reins.

Caro and Thomas broke into laughter.

Thomas was the first to find words. "My darling Caro, I predict our life together will always be full of joy."

Her reply was smothered by his kiss.